The Cornish Mystique

by

Judith Conklin

This is a work of fiction. Names, characters, places, and incidents are either the product of the author's imagination or are used fictitiously, and any resemblance to actual persons living or dead, business establishments, events, or locales, is entirely coincidental.

The Cornish Mystique

COPYRIGHT © 2023 by Judith Conklin

All rights reserved. No part of this book may be used or reproduced in any manner whatsoever without written permission of the author or The Wild Rose Press, Inc. except in the case of brief quotations embodied in critical articles or reviews.
Contact Information: info@thewildrosepress.com

Cover Art by *The Wild Rose Press, Inc.*

The Wild Rose Press, Inc.
PO Box 708
Adams Basin, NY 14410-0708
Visit us at www.thewildrosepress.com

Publishing History
First Edition, 2024
Trade Paperback ISBN 978-1-5092-5489-7
Digital ISBN 978-1-5092-5490-3

Published in the United States of America

Dedication

To the many writers who have helped me along the way, too many to mention,
I most humbly thank you.
Without your advice and opinions,
I would never have become a successful author.
From established authors, to my critique group,
to my beta readers and my editor,
I am indebted to you,
and I fully intend to pay it forward.

Chapter 1

"Cordelia, come back here this instant!" The fan in Lady Delemere's hand fluttered angrily as she watched her daughter flounce out of the room. When the only response she received was a resounding slam from the salon door, her ladyship snapped the fan shut with an irritable flick of her wrist. "Odious child!" she muttered.

The Lady Eugenia, Viscountess Delemere, was not used to having her edicts ignored. Born the pampered daughter and only child of an excessively wealthy and exceedingly snobbish marquis, she had always enjoyed having her slightest dictate obeyed. Even after committing a near fatal *faux pas*, that of marrying Horace Delemere, a lowly viscount with a tainted bloodline and an unfortunate connection to business, she had, through sheer force of will, managed to maintain her dominance over any and all who fell under her shadow. However, it now appeared a perversely obstinate and quite ungrateful child had taken it into her head to question that authority. Well, this was not to be borne!

Her ladyship stiffened her back until she sat rigidly upon the delicate rose damask sofa gracing the richly appointed room. "Really, Phillip," she directed to the one remaining person left in her company, "you simply *must* speak to your sister concerning her conduct of late. I tell you, the silly chit must be brought to heel. And at once!" Raising her chin, she sniffed dramatically. "I vow I simply cannot conceive what has come over her."

The Honorable Phillip Edward Renauld Delemere lounged in one of the comfortable wingback chairs situated next to a sunlit window, his face hidden behind the latest edition of the *Times*. For the past half hour or so, he had given every appearance of being thoroughly engrossed in an article relating the latest antics being played out upon the floor of Parliament. That had not been the case. He had been listening, with no small interest, as his mother and sister engaged in yet another one of their infamous clashes of wills. The skirmish had been amusing to him because he had not been involved and had no inclination to be. But now it appeared his mother was intent upon drawing him into the melee. This unexpected turn did not please him in the least.

He reached for the half-empty glass of sherry resting upon an elegant rosewood table next to his chair, drained its contents, and replaced the stemmed goblet upon the table. His movements were slow and deliberate, for he needed time to search for the right words that would diplomatically extricate him from the position of having to choose sides.

"Phillip? Did you not hear me? Oh, how I do wish you would pay attention when I am speaking to you. In that, you are just like your father."

Phillip slowly folded the newspaper into a neat square, placed it upon the table beside the stemmed goblet, and rose from his chair. "I heard you, Mama."

"Well? What have you to say upon the matter?" his mother prodded imperiously. "Are you, or are you not, going to do as I ask and take Cordelia in hand? She simply *must* be persuaded to immediately abandon her attachment to that…that revolting young man. And she must do so posthaste!" She shifted her rather ample weight upon the comfortable sofa, the gesture emphasizing her displeasure. "This latest misadventure of hers simply must not be allowed to continue, and that is the end of it. Of course, she is just being stubborn about Mr. Cavanaugh because she knows her father and I would never approve of such a match."

Phillip had made his way over to a side table where an array of liquor rested upon a silver tray. Tapping absently upon the stopper of an ornately cut crystal decanter, he considered pouring himself another sherry, then dismissed the idea. Although he wanted another drink badly, and one a great deal more substantial than sherry, he knew from past experience that possessing a clear head was of paramount importance whenever one was about to disoblige his mother. And that is exactly what he was about to do.

In point of fact, Phillip happened to know the young man in question and found no great tragedy in his sister's choice of *beau*. Although not titled, Peter Cavanaugh was, in every way, a refreshingly honest, honorable, and quite amiable young man, not to mention well-padded in the pockets. Many young blades of the aristocracy were not, and judging from the unusual number of bacon-brained fops he had been thrown into contact with of late, Phillip thought Cordelia had shown surprising acumen in choosing to lose her heart to such an appealing young man, titled or not. However, Phillip knew very well that whatever excellent qualities he might assign to young Peter, his endorsement, however exalted, would hold no sway upon his mother. After all, the lofty Lady Eugenia, Viscountess Delemere, considered herself the self-proclaimed *arbiter elegantiarum* for the London *ton*, and she was most particularly conscious of one's position within society. The simple fact that Cavanaugh held no title, with none lurking anywhere within his future, made his suit undeniably and irrevocably unacceptable to any young maiden of rank, never mind the Marquis of Dunsmore's only granddaughter!

Turning toward her, Phillip sighed heavily. "Mama, why must we always indulge in this same conversation every time you and Cordelia have a disagreement? You know very well that I have no jurisdiction over her. I am neither her parent nor her guardian, I am merely her brother. So what is it that continually inspires you to believe I could possibly have any influence over her?"

Her ladyship cast a furious glare at her son. "Please do not vex me further, Phillip. You know perfectly well Cordelia worships you. Now, if only you would have a word with her, I am sure she would listen—"

"Mama, please!" Phillip pulled away from the side table and began a restless prowl about the room. His mother's insistence that he should become embroiled in his sister's latest *affaire du coeur* threw him out of sorts, and he found himself fervently wishing they might find another topic of conversation. "I still do not see…" He paused in front of a small writing desk positioned in front of yet another sunlit window where a number of calling cards, along with several invitations, lay scattered across its glossy surface. He shuffled through them and, finding nothing of particular interest, continued on his way. "As I was saying, I still do not see how I could be of any help in that arena. After all, you must admit my own conduct in the past has been…well, let us just say it has been less than exemplary. And I daresay there are any number of our acquaintances within our sphere of society who would quite willingly claim that is still the case."

"Rubbish," her ladyship bellowed. "Everyone knows young men are allowed a certain margin of freedom that young ladies of quality are not." She sniffed again, this time as if an offensive odor had suddenly filled the room. "It is all part of that dreadful passage into manhood everyone speaks about with such reverence."

Phillip was now in front of the fireplace. He stopped again, placed both hands upon the mantel, and stared down into the remnants of what had once been a cheerful, comforting fire. A strange discontent had joined his restlessness. He wanted to blame his mother's tiresome and incessant prattle for giving rise to the malaise, but he knew the better of it. The sensation was nothing new to him. For some weeks now, nothing seemed to please him. He could find no satisfaction, no interest, in anything; nothing held any importance for him.

"In any event, you have come around quite nicely," his mother was saying. "And rightly so! Unlike that hoyden sister of yours, you have recognized your responsibility to your family and have responded accordingly."

At this point in her discourse, his mother's choler suddenly dissolved into thin air. He knew this because, although he had not bothered to look up, when next she spoke, her voice had taken on a rapturous quality.

"And oh, my dear," she cooed dreamily, "Elise is such a lovely girl. And the daughter of a viscount! Of course, she is not the catch the Marquis of Rotherham's daughter would have been. Now, she is quite the thing, a charming girl…"

"My dear mama…" Phillip groaned. "Rebecca is as

dull as a toad and looks alarmingly like a fish."

Her ladyship began to fan herself again with undue relish. "Well…I must admit she is not overtaxed with a great deal of beauty. Still, it is her breeding that one must take into account. As I am sure you recall, her grandmama…"

Phillip managed to block out his mother's endless chatter. Yes, it was true enough that he had recognized his responsibility to his family. Looking back over the years, he realized he had always done so, even at an early age. Exactly when this recognition had begun, he was not sure, but it was as if he had always known that as the only son of the prestigious Viscountess Delemere and only grandson of the esteemed Marquis of Dunsmore, he had a certain obligation to fulfill. Even during his *rite of passage* years, when he had committed more than his share of mischief, and those years following after, with numerous love affairs and several mistresses… Still, he had never done anything beyond the pale, nothing that would tarnish the exalted lineage from which he had sprung. He had always kept his word, made the correct decision, done the right thing. In short, he had evolved into an honest, respectable, and thoroughly admirable young man—a shining example of what a perfect English gentleman should be. Everyone said so.

"Oh, but now, Elise! She is quite lovely. She will most certainly be an asset to you…"

His mother's mention of Elise Brundridge caused Phillip to bring her to mind. He found himself vaguely surprised that he did not feel the slightest stir of emotion toward Viscount Brundridge's only child. As much as he hated to agree with his mother on any subject, he had to admit that Elise was, indeed, lovely. Small, delicate, and with hair so blonde as to almost be mistaken for silver, a pair of large violet-blue eyes that expressed, quite eloquently, her every mood, and lips…naturally pink, slightly pouting, and always seeming to be in need of kissing…

Phillip frowned. Yes, she was certainly beautiful. So why did he not feel something? Anything, a stirring of blood, a tightening in the groin, any of the normal reactions that naturally followed the prospect of a beautiful woman?

He had been paying his addresses to her since the beginning of the season and, upon their first outing, everyone within the *ton* had immediately declared them a match. She certainly gave every indication of being completely enamored with him. And yet there was something lacking in Elise, something he could not put a name to, but that something had been preventing him from declaring himself.

He was about to turn and admit to his mother, face to face, that he had no intention of ever asking for Elise's hand in marriage, when he became aware of something cool on his fingers. Glancing up, he found his hand resting against a small sculpture. The medium was white marble, almost translucent, with pale pink veining.

He recognized the object immediately, for he had grown up with it occupying one place or another throughout the house, but he had never really looked at it before. Lifting the statue from the mantel, he began to study the sculptor's rendering of a beautiful young peasant girl. One had the feeling she stood on top of a hill, or perhaps a mountain, for the artist had carved both her gown and hair to give the impression of being caught up in a swirling wind. She wore a shawl, also being affected by the wind, and she held a wide, shallow basket, the contents of which was probably heather. It truly was a beautiful piece of art. As his fingers moved over the polished finish, he wondered fleetingly what it would be like to be that free—of duty, of responsibility, of obligation...

"Mama, how did we happen to come into possession of this?"

Her ladyship ceased her fanning and turned. Upon catching sight of the statue, she scowled. "Oh, it is that *wretched* object again. I have repeatedly instructed Daisy to keep it hidden away in some dark corner. But of course Horace *will* find it! He insists that it be placed out in plain sight for any and all to see!" She finished by muttering, "I have no doubt he does so just to annoy me."

Phillip looked surprised. "But why should it annoy you? It is a beautiful piece of work."

His mother replied huffily, "You know very well why it annoys me. It belonged to that...that *gypsy* your grandfather married in what I am certain must have been a moment of complete insanity!"

So that was it. It had belonged to his Grandmama Saoirse. Phillip smiled in spite of himself. No wonder his haughty mother disliked the statue so. It was a glaring reminder of his father's less than immaculate bloodline, diluted as it were with Romany blood. That, and his ownership of a shipping line, however impressive, was a constant source of embarrassment to the unpolluted blue-blooded Lady Eugenia, Viscountess Delemere.

His smile deepened as he recalled the particulars surrounding his grandparent's first meeting with "that gypsy," and their ultimate marriage...

His grandfather, the Honorable Thomas Edward

Delemere, was the fourth son in an aristocratic family with four children. With the positions of heir, military obligation, and servant of the church ably filled by his older siblings, there was nothing else for Thomas to do when he reached his majority except find his own way in the world. He immediately chose the sea. Through the years, he learned much, and by the time he was thirty-five, he was the captain of his own ship, his cargo consisting of anything that would legally turn a profit. One night, in Portsmouth, Captain Delemere decided to visit his favorite inn with nothing more in mind than to partake of a tankard or two of his favorite ale. As happens so frequently in life, he quite unexpectedly partook of something else as well. There, in the middle of the yard, stood a black-eyed Romany girl, as pretty as any man had ever seen, selling trinkets and charms to travelers as they entered the inn. She simply took the captain's breath away. He married her within a week and remained breathless for the rest of his life. It was not until several years after their marriage that a series of fatal familial mishaps unexpectedly propelled him into the position of the new Viscount Delemere. This, in turn, automatically bestowed upon his beautiful wife the lofty status of viscountess.

In a moment of complete insanity? Phillip thought not. For a fleeting moment, he wished he could experience what his grandfather had…to belong only to himself, to go only where his heart led, whether it be in search of adventure upon the high seas or in willing surrender to the promise of paradise found within a pair of bewitching eyes…

The long case clock in the hall, striking out the hour, startled Phillip out of his musing. He glanced at the clock on the mantel. "Blast! Mama, you will have to excuse me." He started toward the door. "I am attending Lady Brundridge's musicale this evening, and I shall be late if I do not hurry."

"One moment, Phillip." His mother rose and faced him. "As you know, your father and I were planning on attending as well. Unfortunately, tonight of all nights, that wretched business your father is so enamored with is preventing that. In recompense, I wonder if you would do me a kindness."

At times, his mother's haughtiness could be infuriating. Phillip fought the urge to point out that the "wretched business" she always referred to with such disparity, the very same shipping company begun by her father-in-law, that lusty sea captain and lover, had been their family's primary source of income for many years, and hopefully would continue to do so for many more years to come. He did not, of course, for he knew the futility of it. Instead, he replied wearily, "Certainly, Mama. What is it?"

"Well...apparently, there is a new inmate within the Brundridge household. A relative, I believe—Hamilton's niece, the vicar's daughter."

Phillip vaguely recalled that Hamilton Brundridge, the sixth member of his family to hold the viscount title, had a younger brother who had become a vicar...in one of the western provinces in England, he thought.

"It seems the vicar has most inconveniently followed his wife in death," his mother was saying, "and there being no other known relatives to take her in, this tatterdemalion has, of course, seen fit to show up upon Brundridge's doorstep. No doubt she plans to endear herself to Hamilton and Isabelle, thereby insinuating herself into a place within the family." Her ladyship patted her elaborate hairstyle, an upswept affair with many intricate curls, as if to verify that every hair was still in place. "Of course, the whole presumption is quite insupportable!"

"Mama," Phillip gently chided. "I can almost guarantee that the good vicar did not purposely leave this world simply to inconvenience Brundridge and his family. Nor do I think he did so in order that his daughter might improve upon her station in life."

"I understand she is a dowdy little thing," his mother continued, as if he had never spoken. "Quite unsuitable, of course, but there it is." She snapped her fan shut once again and began to gently tap her cheek with it. "I was wondering…if you might pay special attention to those in attendance tonight. See if she puts in an appearance."

Phillip groaned. "Oh, Mama, please! Do not ask me to do your spying for you. It simply will not do. I am no good at that sort of thing. I know nothing of gowns, and lace, and, and, all that frippery. If you want to know any particulars about the wretched girl, why do you not simply ask Isabelle? You and she are intimates, after all. I am sure—"

"Isabelle is being quite tight-lipped about the whole affair," his mother interrupted huffily, "which is most unfair of her, to be sure. I have a notion—" Stopping abruptly, she offered Phillip a chilly smile. "Well, never mind about that. Just see what you can find out about her, will you, my dear?"

Phillip said no more. Instead, he turned to flee the room before his mother could think of something else even more repulsive for him to do, when he realized he still held in his hand the small marble sculpture he had removed from the mantel. "Mama, do you mind if I take this with me?" He held up the sculpture.

"Please do," his mother exclaimed, waving a dismissing hand at him. "And you may keep it, so that I may never have to lay my eyes upon it again!"

Once in his room, Phillip found his formal attire had already been plucked from the press. Now it lay upon his bed, neatly arranged by Stanton, his valet. A recent pitcher of hot water, still steaming, had been placed on the washstand, as had fresh towels, soap, and his shaving equipment. Phillip walked over to his bedside table and deposited the marble statue beside his night lamp.

He found himself dreading his evening's commitment, for he knew just how it would be. It would be precisely like so many other past evenings. The music would be excellent, of course. He always enjoyed the music. But afterward? The same people would be there, his peers, all of them, and all of them equally insufferable, discussing the same tired subjects. The women, with their senseless flirtations and mindless chatter. There would be cigars, and liquor—far too much liquor, bragging, swaggering buffoonery, and…Elise.

Removing his jacket, he tossed it onto a nearby chair and began to untie his neckcloth. He was going to have to do something about Elise, he decided, as the neckcloth joined his jacket. They simply would not suit. He began to fumble with the buttons on his silk shirt. But how was he to go about it? He knew very well that a gentleman must never be the one to end a relationship, whether it was an affair or an engagement or merely a simple flirtation. Not if the gentleman wished to remain a gentleman.

Etiquette demanded that it must always be the lady's

choice, at least in appearance. Having shed his shirt, he headed for the washstand. The problem was, how was he to accomplish this if Elise did not wish to end their association? And he was almost certain she would not. He gingerly rinsed his face in the overly warm water, then, because of the late hour, instead of calling for Stanton to shave him he prepared to shave himself. As he slathered soap on his face, his thoughts focused on yet another—although closely related—dilemma. How in the world was he to pacify his mother once she discovered Elise was not destined to be her daughter-in-law?

Chapter 2

Bethany Brundridge sat at the window of her third-floor bedchamber, gazing out into the night. She sat in complete darkness except for the moonlight spilling into the room. Every now and then she could hear snatches of beautiful music, tinkling laughter, and clinking glasses carried aloft by a soft breeze. She listened intently for a few moments before closing her eyes and imagining the scene downstairs.

The room would be aglow in soft candlelight. Scores of elegant ladies, dressed in lovely gowns and with fans fluttering, would be speaking gaily to an equal number of handsome young bucks. Servants, too, were in attendance. They would be gliding skillfully through the crowded room, balancing large silver trays laden with drinks and delicious tidbits of every kind. Her aunt and uncle were no doubt strolling among their guests, making pleasant conversation, and seeing to it that no one was in want of anything. And then, of course, Elise would be there, stunningly beautiful as usual.

Bethany opened her eyes to stare out of the window once again. As lights from the neighboring townhouse winked at her through a lacy barrier of tree leaves, she wondered vaguely how many other parties were being given that night, just like the one downstairs. She quickly dismissed such an absurd notion. No one of any importance, at least none within the aristocracy, would dare plan such an amusement on the same night as one of Viscountess Brundridge's galas.

A twinge of envy swept over her until she remembered her gown. Instinctively, she looked down in the dimness and began to smooth out the well-worn folds in her lap. It was the best of her three dresses. She remembered that at one time it had been rather pretty. But no longer. The rich blue shade it had been in the beginning was now nothing more than a watery blue due to an endless number of washings. And the frayed edges at the neck and cuffs could no longer be mended or hidden. Even if she had been graciously included in the festivities tonight, she realized she could not have attended. At its best, the gown was not appropriate for the occasion being enjoyed below. Downhearted, she placed her head on the windowsill just as another wisp of music drifted into the room.

She had not been there but a moment when there came the rapid clang of metal against glass. The music stopped and the sound of her uncle's raised voice filtered into her window. He began by thanking his guests for accepting their invitations to such an auspicious occasion as was scheduled for tonight. Then, in the most elaborate terms, he launched into the particulars promised by this evening's entertainment.

Apparently, the guest of honor was a well-known but brash composer. Some labeled him an upstart, a scandalous creature who was poisoning the world of music with his very licentious brand of music. Others claimed him to be a genius, his melodies enchanting. Many, it was said, had embraced his compositions to the point of obsession. Bethany had never heard of him or his music, but her aunt and uncle, and yes, even Elise, had all been elated at their achievement in securing his appearance at their soiree. His name, her uncle theatrically announced, was Johann Strauss II.

Suddenly, Bethany could not stand being confined to her room any longer. She quickly abandoned her seat by the window, grabbed her shawl, and hurried for the door.

She silently slipped down the back stairs, passed unnoticed through the busy kitchen, and stepped out of the servant's entrance. Within seconds, she had disappeared into the darkness.

****

Phillip brought his highflyer to a skidding halt in front of Hamilton Brundridge's townhouse and absently tossed the reins down to the lackey who had rushed out to meet him. He was late in arriving for the Brundridge's soiree and that only added to his choler. Elise, Phillip was sure, would be in one of her tiresome little pouts because of it, and the mere thought of his having to deal with her mood almost caused him to turn around and head for his club. Dammit, he did not want to be there, but there was no help for it. Good manners dictated that he must put in an appearance. Grabbing his hat, he jumped down from his high perch and hurried to the door.

The Brundridge's long-time footman, Bates, immediately answered Phillip's knock.

"Good evening, Bates," Phillip said cheerfully as he stepped into the hall. "I hope all is well with you."

"I am quite well, sir," Bates replied. "Thank you for asking. May I take your things?"

Phillip had no sooner relinquished his hat, coat and gloves than Elise appeared in a doorway a short distance

The Cornish Mystique

down the hall and floated toward him.

Phillip expected her to look lovely and she did not disappoint. Her face was that of an angel, and her hair was styled to perfection with not a curl out of place. Her figure, which any man would find desirable, was sheathed in the traditional white gown that all young ladies wore during their coming-out season. But this gown had been artfully, and very generously, embellished with tiny crystal beads so that she literally sparkled with every movement. He also did not fail to notice that her décolletage had been cut dangerously low.

Phillip studied her as she approached, wondering once again why he felt no response to her beauty.

"Mr. Delemere, you are here at last!" she called, smiling prettily.

Phillip bowed in her direction. "Good evening, Miss Brundridge. You look lovely tonight, as usual."

But then…it happened. Just before she reached him, that disapproving, predictable pout appeared on her beautiful face. "Thank you for your compliment, Mr. Delemere. You are most gallant. But I must say, sir, that you have given me such a fright." She captured his arm, and they began to drift toward the reception rooms.

Phillip raised an eyebrow. "Oh? How so?"

"Well, I was quite worried that something was amiss and that you would not be putting in an appearance tonight." Her pout deepened into that of a churlish child, complete with bottom lip extended. "I would have been devastated if that had been the case."

"Pray, forgive me," he responded politely. "Actually, my mother had something to discuss with me. I am afraid time got away."

Elise's eyes immediately lit up and instead of

continuing on to the reception rooms where the other guests were situated, she gently guided him into the softly lit library. "Oh, dear," she mewled, quietly closing the door behind them, "I do hope it had nothing to do with Cordelia. I am sure you know there has been talk…" Even in the dimness, Phillip was certain he saw a small smirk form at the corners of her delectable mouth. "I believe his name is Cavanaugh, is it not? Peter Cavanaugh? They say she met him at Henrietta Leighton's coming-out party." She stamped a tiny foot. "On my word! I am still beside myself for missing dear Henrietta's party and, therefore, missing all the excitement!"

As she was speaking, Phillip had strolled over to a large desk and turned up the flame of an oil lamp resting upon its shiny surface. He recognized this detour into the library for what it was, a fishing expedition. And if he was the fat trout, he wanted to make sure he had a clear view of the angler.

"I am sorry to disappoint you, Elise," he offered, returning to her, "but I know nothing about Henrietta Leighton's coming-out party. I did not attend that gala. And I am not in the least interested in any of Cordelia's whims. I cannot imagine why you, or anyone else, for that matter, would think so."

Phillip was surprised to see Elise turn pink. He had not believed she would recognize a rebuff. She certainly was not used to them.

"Oh, of course not! I mean… I hope you did not think—"

"But as long as we are on the subject of gossip, I understand that you have acquired a new member within your household. A relative of some kind, I believe?"

Elise literally withered before him. "Yes," she replied sullenly. "Poor Mama is quite undone because of it, too. I told her it was only a matter of time before the whole population of London became aware of it. She tried to tell Father what an embarrassment it would be, but he would not listen."

Phillip frowned. "I am sorry, but apparently I am a bit dimwitted. Why would such an acquisition to your household be considered an embarrassment?"

"Oh, Phillip dear, I realize that you are just being kind, but really, it is such an embarrassment to have her in residence."

"Why?" Phillip prodded. "And by the way, what is her name?"

"Her name is Bethany, and she is a cousin on father's side of the family. Her father was papa's brother. Honestly, she is such a dreary little thing! Her gowns are quite shabby and outdated, as well. She is from the country, you know, so she possesses none of the social graces. Why, she has never even had a governess, for heaven's sake!"

Phillip found Elise's reaction to her cousin not only surprising but rather hateful. He was, of course, already aware of the circumstances for her cousin's unexpected arrival, and it seemed to him that Elise would, or should, feel at least a little compassion for her. But for the grace of God, the roles might well have been reversed. It could have been Elise standing at the good vicar's doorstep in her bedazzled gown asking for a bed and bread.

"Am I to assume, then, that this cousin of yours, because of her unsuitable wardrobe, as well as her less than perfect deportment, will not be in attendance tonight?"

"No, she will most certainly *not* be in attendance tonight." Elise began to tap a delicate lace fan against her free palm as she paced back and forth in front of him. "It is bad enough that Uncle John should choose to die right in the midst of my coming-out season! I mean, it has put a pall on absolutely everything. Papa insists that we should cancel the remaining plans concerning my coming-out this year. He feels it would be in poor taste to participate in such a festive occasion when we should be in mourning. He promises that I may have another come-out next year. But, thank goodness, Mama will not hear of it. And why should we go into mourning? Mama and I did not even know the man!" She stopped, snapped open her fan, and began to wave it frantically in front of her face. "And besides all of that, I don't even look good in black. And now, we have this…this very unsuitable creature foisted upon us… I tell you, it is unconscionable!"

As she was unleashing her tirade, Phillip had wandered back to the desk supporting the now brightly lit oil lamp and settled against the edge of its solid frame. He lounged there now, his feet crossed at the ankles and his arms folded across his chest.

"I understand her arrival is a surprise to all of you, Elise," he replied quietly. "And I understand that tonight may not be the proper time to introduce her to the *ton*. But I do not believe it is as bad as you think. Perhaps, in the coming days, you might help her along in adjusting to her new life. I'm sure she would be very grateful, and I think it would be quite nice of you. You, of all people, could groom her as to the proper manners required of a genteel young lady. And as to her wardrobe, why don't you give her some of your already worn gowns? You have no use for them anymore, and certainly no one will remember seeing them on you, not with you present and wearing some new confection."

Elise abruptly stopped her pacing and, for the first time Phillip could recall, she actually glared at him.

"I most certainly shall not! Those are *my* gowns, and they shall remain so. And as for the rest of what you suggest, that will not be necessary. In a very short time, she will no longer be with us."

"Oh?"

She renewed her pacing. "Even as we speak, Mama has put into motion plans to find Bethany employment. Mama has heard of a wealthy woman who has recently been given the responsibility of raising her four young grandchildren. It seems their parents were killed in a carriage accident. We do not think the woman will be too particular about a governess, since she is quite elderly and is desperately in need of help. Mama has already written to her, and we are simply waiting for her answer."

Somehow, Phillip could not credit Hamilton Brundridge's approval with the sort of treatment being inflicted upon his niece. Phillip liked Viscount Brundridge very much and found him to be a kind, unassuming, and very fair gentleman. Much like Phillip's own father.

"And I suppose your father agrees with the two of you to have her elsewhere?"

"Oh, goodness, no. Papa does not know anything about our plan. For some quite peculiar reason, Papa thinks it is his sworn duty to keep her under his roof and care for her permanently. No, he knows nothing. If he did, I am sure he would put up quite a fuss."

"Yes, I am certain he would," Phillip muttered. He paused, digesting what he had just heard, then continued. "So…I suppose I am to assume that this employment is sufficiently far enough away as to prevent any association between your cousin and the family?"

Elise came to an abrupt halt, her lips twisting wickedly. "Quite," she cooed. "It is in Ireland!"

Phillip had had enough! He stood up. "Elise, I hope you will excuse me. I am certain time is short, and I would very much like to enjoy a cigar before this evening's entertainment begins."

Her sweet smile was back in place. "But of course. I understand perfectly. You gentlemen are all alike in that you cannot seem to resist your cigars or your port."

****

The moment Phillip stepped out onto the lawn, he felt a tremendous sense of relief. Just being away from Elise was liberating. But being with her had been enlightening, as well, because…now, he knew! It was like an epiphany—a sudden awareness that had eluded him for weeks. It was so clear now why he had never been able to feel anything for Elise. It was her unbridled selfishness, her arrogance, but most of all it was the depth of her cunning. Oh, she had hidden it well, but tonight he was finally able to recognize the ugliness behind that beautiful facade!

He paused just long enough to light a cigar, then continued his leisurely stroll across the lawn. The night was lovely. A soft, warm breeze whispered across the grass and occasionally swelled into a strong gust that set the trees and shrubs dancing and the fireflies dipping and swirling. There was almost a full moon overhead, but not bright enough yet to fade the stars. They cluttered the sky like millions of diamonds scattered across a black velvet throw.

He had not gone far when he happened upon several large shrubs positioned along a meandering cobblestoned path. It looked as if it curved around the side of the house. Curious as to where it might lead, he stepped onto the path and began to follow its course.

****

Bethany had settled at her favorite place in the Brundridge yard, a small rose garden, not too distant from the side of the house. It was her favorite place, not because the roses were lovely, or that it was well shaded, or that there were several benches placed within the rows where one could sit and admire the flowers. It was because no one else ever went there.

She sat on her most visited bench, which was placed in the middle of an arbor blanketed with climbing roses. As she twirled a perfect little rosebud in her fingers, she listened to the laughter and music coming from within the house.

"Good evening."

Startled, Bethany jumped up and whirled around.

The deep, resonant voice belonged to a very tall gentleman. He was standing in the shadows, but she could tell he was dressed in evening attire. This meant, of course, that he was one of the guests.

"Oh! Please excuse me. "I...I..." She frantically looked around to see if there were any others about. She did not see anyone else. "I am very sorry. I did not expect anyone would be here." She turned and started to scurry off.

"Just a moment, please."

His deep, commanding voice caused her to stop. She

slowly turned back to face him.

Tossing away his cigar, he stepped out of the shadows and walked toward her, not stopping until he was right in front of her, and very, very close to her. "I believe you have it backward," he murmured. "It is I who should be apologizing to you rather than the reverse." He held a fully opened rose in his hand and he brushed her chin with its petals. "I did not mean to startle you. I'm sorry."

Bethany knew she should acknowledge his apology, but she could not. Her lips, her tongue, her throat, even her lungs had become paralyzed. All she could do was stare up into the most beautiful pair of eyes she had ever seen. Indeed, everything about the gentleman was beautiful.

He had thick hair, black as pitch, and with just enough curl as to give him a slightly mussed, carefree appearance. Beautifully shaped dark brows, onyx eyes, exquisitely shaped nose, jaw, and a full, expressive mouth were all encased in skin that any woman would envy. He was, in fact, the most handsome man she had ever seen.

Smiling, he brushed the rose across her cheek. "I hope you will accept this rose as an apology. I know it isn't much, and it doesn't even belong to me, but it's all I have at the moment as recompense for disturbing you."

Bethany swallowed with difficulty. Her mouth and throat were as dry as a desert. "I…uh…of course. Yes." She took the rose that was still resting against her cheek. "Of course, I accept your apology. And…thank you."

In the moonlight she saw him raise a brow, askance.

"For the rose, I mean." She licked her lips nervously. "Well, if you will excuse me, I must go now."

Again, she turned to leave, but again he stopped her, this time by catching her arm. "Wait a moment. Please. Why are you so skittish? Have I, perhaps, interrupted some sort of clandestine meeting?"

She looked at him pleadingly. "No, of course not. It is just that…well, I should not be here. But I did not think anyone would be out in the garden with the party in progress, and…the night is so lovely…I only came out to get some fresh air." She tugged against his grip. "Please, I really must go now."

"Not yet. I want to get a good look at you."

He pulled her out into the moonlight. He knew she was a beauty. Even in the dappled shading he could see, and even sense, a breathless kind of beauty that Elise, with her polished and tightly controlled perfection, could never achieve. This young woman was small, slender, and yet there were delicious-looking curves her gown could not hide. Her raven hair looked soft as silk. And because she wore it loose and free, delicate curls caught in the wind to float around her face. In spite of himself, Phillip reached up and caught a handful of riotous curls. They were soft as down! Her eyes were large and very dark, and he suspected that in the light they would be as dark as his. Her nose, perfectly shaped, and her mouth… It took everything he had not to kiss her.

Now he understood Elise's haste in permanently sending her cousin as far away as possible.

"You are Bethany, are you not?" he murmured. It was a question he already knew the answer to.

Bethany simply nodded because she could not do anything else. He still held her arm, and his other hand remained buried in her hair.

Finally, she found her voice. "Y-…yes. I am

Bethany. But please!" She tried to pull free. "Please, do not tell anyone you saw me. They would be very angry, and I...am their guest. I meant no harm."

Phillip reluctantly let her go, and she scrambled a short distance away before suddenly stopping. She turned and faced him. At that precise moment, a strong gust of wind blew across the lawn and caught in her skirt, causing it to billow out. It did the same to her shawl, and her hair became an explosion of swirling curls.

"Excuse me, but who are you?" she asked. "And how did you know my name?"

Phillip barely heard her, for he was finding it hard to breathe and he was certain his heart would stop beating at any moment. As he stared at Bethany, the beautiful marble statue of the girl standing in the wind filled his brain. It was Bethany! Except for the basket of heather, it was her image, down to the last detail, resting on his nightstand.

Then, his brain registered another image, that of a vibrant young sea captain as his eyes took in a wildly beautiful gypsy girl for the first time.

It took Phillip several tries before he was able to speak. "My name is Philip Delemere," he finally replied, "and I was told about you."

Chapter 3

Phillip awakened the next morning bleary eyed, having spent most of the night tossing and turning in an attempt to go to sleep. When he did find sleep, he had been plagued with dreams of Bethany—of soft hair tangled in his fingers, her sweet, inviting mouth, and eyes that could cause a man to melt. Rolling over, he haphazardly stuffed his pillow more firmly under his head as, once again, the events of the previous evening began to haunt him.

After Bethany had disappeared into the night, he had not remained long at the Brundridge's musicale. He did stay for the concert. Decorum demanded it. Afterward, he managed to tolerate a few minutes of mingling with his peers. Deportment demanded that. But after only one drink, one cigar, and perhaps twenty minutes of inane conversation, he remembered feeling as if he could not endure another moment in the presence of such an arrogant group of buffoons. An added irritant had been Elise. She had clung to his arm, claiming him as her own, smothering him with her possessiveness when all the while he wished it were Bethany at his side. He had been about to toss decorum and deportment out the window by making a rude exit, when, as luck would have it, he spied a good friend of his across the crowded room.

Adam Westcott, destined to inherit the title of baron upon his father's demise, had been a classmate of his at

Eton. Their friendship had begun there and continued on when both had chosen to finish up their studies at Cambridge University. They had shared many an escapade during those years, some with ladies of dubious reputations. Upon seeing his friend, Phillip quickly recognized a way out of his miserable situation.

Adam had often declared that he owed his friend a great debt, dating back to a certain night several years earlier in Covent Garden. It involved a delightful stage actress and her unexpected, unpleasant, and quite unforgiving suitor. A gun had discharged, and there had been a mad scramble, with Phillip stuffing his inebriated friend out a window. Although it was never stated, Phillip had always suspected that the true debt occurred, not when he pushed Adam out the window to safety, but when Phillip had judiciously remembered to grab Adam's trousers as he exited the same window. Considering the mood he was in, Phillip decided there would never come a better time in which to call in his marker.

He managed to catch his friend's eye and, when Adam wandered over, Phillip gave him *that look*. It was a signal for needing aid that the two had used for years.

"Adam! What a pleasure to see you. It has been quite a while."

Both men, smiling, shook hands.

"My dear Phillip, yes indeed, it has. I have been away, up in the northland helping my father with some business affairs. I've only been back a fortnight." As expected, Adam's appreciative eyes swept over Elise. "I, uhhhh, rather expected to see you at Miss Leighton's coming-out party a week or so past, but apparently you were not in attendance that evening."

Phillip had looked dutifully remorseful. "Yes, well, I am afraid I was otherwise indisposed..." He doubted his friend even heard his reply, for Adam was by then unabashedly admiring Elise's icy beauty. Phillip had gently pressed Elise toward Adam. "Oh, pray forgive my manners. Miss Brundridge, may I introduce you to an old friend of mine, the Honorable Mister Adam Westcott. Adam, allow me to introduce to you the Honorable Miss Elise Brundridge."

Elise had gracefully raised a delicate hand and Adam, quickly taking possession of her dainty fingers, had bowed over them. "Miss Brundridge, it is, indeed, a great honor to make your acquaintance."

By that time, there was only one more obstacle to overcome. Did Adam already have an encumbrance for the evening? Phillip had looked around curiously. "And which lovely debutante are you escorting tonight, my friend? Pray, where is the young lady, and do I know her?"

Coloring slightly, Adam had confessed, "Actually, I am alone this evening. I was to have had the honor of escorting the Honorable Miss Caroline Woodbridge to this evening's gala, but she became ill quite suddenly this very afternoon. They fear it was the poached salmon she was served at luncheon. I believe the doctor is attending her, even as we speak."

"Ahhhhh," Phillip sighed, and when a convenient pause occurred in the conversation, he tugged uncomfortably at his collar and turned toward Elise. "Miss Brundridge, I pray you must forgive me... I was not going to say anything, but... Well, the truth of the matter is, I am not feeling very well myself. If I did not know the better of it, it would seem as if I had joined

Miss Woodbridge at luncheon—which, I assure you, was not the case. But...I think, perhaps, I should take my leave. Indeed, I am beginning to feel quite ill."

The powers that be had apparently been with Phillip because he began to perspire—not because he was ill, but because the room was overcrowded with guests, and the confined space had become quite warm.

Adam looked genuinely concerned. "I say, old chap, you do look a bit peaked. Perhaps you should go. And please do not worry about Miss Brundridge. I should be more than happy to attend her for the rest of the evening. I assure you, she will be in good hands."

After that, it was only a matter of collecting his hat, gloves, and coat, and Phillip was out the door.

He decided on his way home that he was behaving like an untried young pup! Yes, Bethany Brundridge was a truly beautiful young woman, and in an extremely exciting and stimulating way. But then, so were many others. Elise certainly had her charms, and he could name many more. No, his strange discontent had nothing to do with his reaction to the fairer sex—or with the lack of it. He had just grown tired of the London scene in general. Its hypocrisy. Its arrogance. Its meaningless existence. He just needed a change of scenery, some peace and quiet without all the pretense exhibited so freely within his social rank.

By the time he arrived home, he had begun to form a plan that would neatly and permanently extricate him from his terrible malady.

A soft knock on his door roused him from his troubled sleep.

"Enter," he growled, and rolled over to face a piercing shaft of sunlight which had found a crack in the draperies.

A maid, carrying his usual morning tray of coffee, cream, and sugar, opened the door.

"Just put the tray on the table by the window, Dora. I will serve myself. Thank you... Oh, and tell Stanton that I will not be needing him this morning. I will attend myself."

Half an hour later, freshly shaven and dressed for the day, Phillip walked into the dining room. His father was alone at the table, a plate with a smattering of leftover eggs and a half-eaten scone before him. His face, however, was hidden behind the open pages of the London *Times*.

Phillip headed for the sideboard. "Good morning, sir."

Horace Delemere peeked around the paper. "Good morning, my boy."

Quickly filling his plate, Phillip settled at the table to the right of his father. "Has anything of interest happened in the world that I should know about? I ask because you do not look especially pleased by what you have been reading."

Viscount Delemere rustled the paper in an irritable gesture. "I tell you, Phillip, this country is going to ruin. Why, the paper is full of nothing but economic disaster, and there is a wave of crime sweeping this country that is astonishing." He gave the newspaper another irritable shake. "And it is no better in Ireland. It is not surprising, knowing the Irish. Still, since that dreadful Potato Rebellion has been put to rest, you would think those heathens would have the sense to settle down a bit. But no. Now they have embraced that ridiculous Fenian Movement, and it is growing by leaps and bounds. Some of their leaders have been rightly put away, but that hasn't dampened their ardor one bit. And to put a topper on it, I have just read an article about some fiend, running loose in Ireland, kidnapping and killing young women. And the authorities seem to believe he is not alone. They think he has a following, and there is some sort of ritual involved."

Phillip attempted to make a comment, but his father merely took a breath and continued his tirade.

"And now Palmerston! By Jove, there is a muddle for you. What he plans to do about the Irish is something both Derby and Disraeli are watching closely, to be sure. I tell you, my boy, I thank God every day that He gave me the good sense to stay out of politics."

Phillip, busily buttering a scone, smiled and nodded. "I agree with you there, sir. I also agree with your assessment of the country going to ruin, especially London." He finished buttering the scone, but instead of taking a bite, he replaced the bun on his plate. "As a matter of fact, that brings me to a point I would like to discuss with you."

There must have been something in Phillip's tone that caught his father's attention. Viscount Delemere immediately closed the paper and placed it beside his plate, his interest in England's imminent demise suddenly forgotten.

"Certainly, dear boy. Is something amiss?"

"Well, yes and no. The truth of the matter is, I have been thinking, for some time now, that I would like to get out of London. I seem to need a change. I have been thinking of taking up residence at Gull Haven."

"Gull Haven? But...why, Phillip? Are you so unhappy here?"

Phillip nodded. "Yes, sir, I am. Oh, I really do not know how to say it. I suppose I have just outgrown London. There is nothing here for me anymore. All this dashing about is wearing thin, and I would very much like to settle into a more sedate, quiet way of life. And after all, Grandmamma Saoirse did will Gull Haven to me. It just seems a shame that the place should sit there vacant year after year." Phillip suddenly scowled. "Gad, it sounds as if I have entered my dotage, does it not?"

"At still on the shy side of thirty? I doubt that." His father chuckled. "Well, of course that is up to you, and, as you say, the place is yours. But, Phillip, it must be in wicked shape by now. Heavens, Gull Haven has been standing vacant for what must be well over ten years or more. And with the place facing the open sea and literally clinging onto the edge of one of those Cornish cliffs, do you suppose it is even habitable?"

Phillip shook his head. "No, no. I would not think it should be in too bad a shape. It is embedded in solid granite, as you well know, and I have had a caretaker there for some years now. He and his wife have been looking after the place, and I have gotten regular reports from him through the years as to what needed to be repaired and to the general shape of the place."

"But what will you do there? It is so remote, Phillip. How will you occupy your time?"

Phillip took a generous sip of his coffee. "I have been thinking about that, and I have decided to try and make it a working estate, at least to some extent. I understand that sheep and cattle can stand the climate quite well. Another plus is, I would be closer to my mining investments, although I am thinking of selling my interests." He smiled faintly. "Let us face it, Father,

I cannot live for the rest of my life on my inheritance. It will eventually run out. And I certainly cannot allow you to continue to support me. By that I mean I cannot, in all good conscience, continue to live in your home and eat the food that you provide. I am a grown man, and at some point, I must become independent."

His father sighed. "Well, I can certainly see where you have thought it out. In all honesty, I envy you. As you know, I was never one to go in for all this society foolishness. I, myself, would have liked very much to reside somewhere quietly. But, well, your mother wanted the excitement and gaiety of the big city, so of course, we have always lived here."

Phillip, leaning toward his father, murmured, "That brings up another point, sir. I would very much appreciate it if you would not share the particulars of this discussion with Mama. At least, not for the moment. Not until I see how things are in Cornwall. And there are other…matters…that I must see to before my plans are made known."

Viscount Delemere sat up abruptly. "Oh, my, yes! Your mother! Oh, dear boy, your mother will not be at all obliging to this idea of yours. No, no. Not at all! And, and…what of Miss Brundridge!"

"As to Miss Brundridge," Phillip muttered sourly, "that is one of the other matters I must see to. And I fear I must do so as soon as possible."

"But Phillip… Oh, dear me, surely you do not nourish the hope that Miss Brundridge would be agreeable to embrace such a lifestyle as you are planning? Why, she is used to London! With all its delights. I am sorry, dear boy, but I cannot imagine—"

"It is immaterial whether Miss Brundridge will be

agreeable or not. You see, I have no intention of ever sharing my life with Miss Brundridge. Not now or ever."

Phillip tossed his napkin next to his plate of half-eaten eggs and rose abruptly. He checked his watch. "You must excuse me, sir, as I have a number of things that I must accomplish today, and it seems that time is passing rather quickly."

"Certainly, but—"

"And that reminds me..." Phillip grabbed the freshly buttered scone off his plate. "I must inform Cook that I will not be dining in tonight, nor will I be in residence for several days to come." Taking a generous bite out of the scone, he started for the door.

"Phillip, wait! Where are you off to?"

Phillip stopped in the doorway, swallowed the bite of scone he had taken, and faced his father. "Right now, I must have a quick word with Stanton; then, I have a few errands that I must see to. After that, sir, I shall be heading for Cornwall. Posthaste."

In truth, Phillip had a long list of commissions, all neatly organized in his head. His first stop was to his bank, where he arranged to have a large amount of funds transferred to a bank in Cornwall nearest to his estate. Next came a quick visit to his solicitor, one to his tailor, to his club, where he paid off his tab and, lastly, to the residence of Viscount Brundridge. This was a courtesy call he was loath to make. Still, if he were to remain a gentleman, Phillip knew it was necessary.

Bates, of course, opened the door.

"Good afternoon, Bates," Phillip said affably. "Is Miss Brundridge, by any chance, free to see me this afternoon?"

"I am sorry, sir, but Miss Brundridge is not in at the

moment."

"Oh? Well, do you know when she might be expected back?"

"I really could not say, sir. Both Miss Brundridge and her ladyship have gone out for the day. Would you care to leave a message?"

Phillip frowned. He hated to just leave a written note informing Elise of his hasty departure. That seemed rather unchivalrous considering what the inevitable intent would mean. He was about to tell Bates he would return later when he had a thought.

"Bates, would you see if Miss Bethany Brundridge will receive me?"

Bates' eyebrow rose ever so slightly, although his facial expression never wavered. "Of course, sir. If you will please step this way, I will announce you to Miss Brundridge."

Phillip was left standing in the entrance hall feeling for all the world as if he were calling on a young lady for the first time. It was a mixture of nervousness and anticipation that he had not felt in years, and he found it almost comical that he should do so now. What in heaven's name was the matter with him? She was, after all, just a mere slip of a girl—of no consequence. The daughter of a lowly vicar and certainly of no import. She possessed no breeding, no social rank, and she certainly held no great fortune... What was it about the wretched girl?

Presently, Bates returned and led him into the parlor with the explanation that Miss Brundridge would be down shortly.

After some minutes, which Phillip spent pacing up and down, the parlor door opened and the girl he had met in the moonlight entered the room, carrying several books in her arms. At once, the entire atmosphere seemed to come alive, and he immediately felt that same sense of electricity he had experienced in the garden.

"Mr. Delemere? Good afternoon." She curtsied prettily. "Are...are you certain it is me you wish to see?" she asked hesitantly.

Phillip could not stop staring at her. There she was, just as he had seen her the night before, except now it was daylight. Everything he had seen in the moonlight was still there, only more so. Now, he saw that she did have dark eyes, black as midnight, and they held an expression of complete innocence. To his amazement, he realized the expression was natural. There was not an ounce of pretense about the girl. And of even more importance, she was completely unaware of its effect on people. He was certain of it.

"Mr. Delemere?" she repeated. "Did you wish to see me?"

He was startled out of his stupor. "Yes, Miss Brundridge. I hope I have not inconvenienced you by asking for an audience." Her cheeks turned a delicate shade of pink, reminding Phillip of the rose he had given her the night before. They were exactly the same shade!

"Not...not at all, sir, although I cannot imagine why you would want to see me."

Phillip watched as she quickly placed the books on a small table, then clasped her hands in front of her so hard that her knuckles were turning white. Phillip immediately knew why. She was terrified of Elise finding out about this meeting...of their being alone together.

"I was certain Mr. Bates had made a mistake when

he said you requested to see me, but he said no, that you had specifically asked for me."

She hurried to a chair opposite the sofa, sat down and indicated that he take a seat facing her.

Phillip smiled, noting that she had taken a seat that would carefully avoid any contact between the two of them. "Actually, I came to see your cousin," he explained, settling on the sofa, "but when Bates told me she was not in, I thought of you. You see, something has come up, and I will be leaving shortly for Cornwall. I came by to tell Miss Brundridge that I would be away for a while and to apologize to her for leaving so early last evening."

"Di…did you say…Cornwall?"

Phillip noticed that her face had drained of all color. Then, slowly, her features regained their rose-like warmth. "Yes, Cornwall," he replied, somewhat puzzled. "You see, I have inherited a small estate on the Cornish coast, and I am planning to move there."

Bethany was barely listening. Her heart was pounding so that she feared it might burst at any moment. This was the tall figure who had stepped out of the shadows the night before, who had caressed her cheek with the petals of a rose, and who had threaded his fingers in her hair. This was the entity who had captured her with little more than the sound of his voice and the velvet strength of his grip on her arm. This was the man who had filled her dreams during the night…and this same man was moving to Cornwall. Her Cornwall!

Bethany was jarred back to reality when she remembered that this was the very same man who was betrothed to Elise.

"…I am hoping not too many repairs will be

necessary before I am able to take up residence." Phillip leaned forward and softened his voice. "Please forgive me, but I could not help noticing your reaction when I mentioned Cornwall. May I ask the reason for such a response?"

She smiled ever so slightly. "I was born in Cornwall, Mr. Delemere, and I lived there all my life until…well, until my father died, and I was required to come here. It was my home," she finished softly.

Easing back on the sofa, Phillip completed her sentence. "And you are missing being there."

"Yes. Everything I love and cherish is there."

"I'm sorry," he murmured. Then he quickly returned to business. He rose from the sofa. "Well, I really must be going. The hour is getting late, and I still have a number of things to attend to."

Bethany rose from her seat as well. As she did so, Phillip bowed and took her hand. He placed a light kiss on her fingers. "Thank you for seeing me, Miss Brundridge. I would ask one thing of you, if I may. I would appreciate it very much if you would not mention the specific reason for my trip to Cornwall…to either your cousin or to your aunt and uncle, for that matter. That information, I think, should come directly from me."

Bethany straightened her shoulders, lifted her chin, and answered with what she hoped was a steady voice. "Of course, Mr. Delemere. I assume, however, that you do wish me to tell my cousin that you—"

"What on earth is going on here!" Elise shrieked as she stormed into the room. "Really, Bethany, however did you get the notion that you may receive our guests during our absence? I realize that you were raised in the country and are therefore sadly lacking in social procedures, but you are quite presumptuous to assume my place in this house. It is just a blessing that Mama and I have returned at this moment. Otherwise, we would have never known of your aggressive nature. Now, please excuse yourself and leave immediately. I am quite certain Mama will have a few words to say to you regarding this matter."

Bethany had become rooted to the floor when Elise burst into the room. Now, Phillip watched as she stood there in shocked silence, looking at her cousin like a trapped little fawn with nowhere to run.

After a moment's hesitation, Bethany slowly turned to him. "I…hope you will please pardon my impertinence, Mr. Delemere, and that you will excuse me now." She hurried from the room.

Phillip stood there, stunned, glaring at Elise. "That was completely unnecessary, Elise," he finally muttered between clenched teeth.

Elise simply smiled. "On the contrary, Phillip dear. It is high time Bethany learns her place within this house before she begins to take on airs. It is bad enough that we are plagued by her presence, without having to endure her impertinence. I can assure you, this sort of thing will not happen again."

"It certainly will not," Phillip uttered icily, "at least not where I am concerned. Elise, I think you should know that your cousin has been nothing but gracious to me, and she in no way tried to assume your position. I specifically asked to see her. Not you, or your mother, or the scullery maid. I very plainly requested an audience with Miss Bethany Brundridge. Now, if you will excuse me, I feel the need for some fresh air. I have given your cousin a message to give you. You can get it from her. Good afternoon to you, Miss Brundridge."

He strode from the room without looking back.

Once outside, Phillip realized he was shaking with anger. How, in the name of heaven, did he ever, for an instant, think that marriage to Elise could be a pleasant experience? Why had he been unable to see the callousness in her before? And why did he see it so clearly now? If he had any doubts about leaving London previously, he certainly did not have them any longer. He could not wait to be rid of them all. And that poor girl, he thought miserably, what would become of Bethany in that house of witches? He could walk away from them, and was doing so, but she could not. She was a captive there, at least for a while. He relaxed then, as he recalled Elise saying Isabelle was waiting for confirmation on some employment she had arranged for Bethany. She would be free of them then, he thought happily as he mounted his horse and rode away.

Chapter 4

Phillip immediately returned home after leaving the Brundridge residence. Before he left that morning, he had instructed Stanton, his valet, to pack him a satchel with enough clothing for three to four days. He had also sent a message to the mews to have a freshly fed and watered horse ready for travel. He expected to collect his luggage, change to the fresh horse, and quickly be on his way to Cornwall, without having to make any further explanations to anyone. He should have known better.

As he entered the back door and made his way through the house, several servants nervously approached and announced that he was expected immediately in the library. Phillip cursed his bad luck, sensing that the command could only have been issued by his mother. Somehow, she had become aware of his plans. He had hoped this confrontation could have waited until his plans were, if not completely finalized, at the very least well under way.

He knocked twice before opening the library door and stepping inside.

Cordelia sat on the softly upholstered sofa, busily at work on a needlepoint sampler. His mother, however, rapidly paced back and forth in front of her daughter.

"Good afternoon, ladies," Phillip said pleasantly. "I understand my presence has been requested."

Stopping abruptly, his mother whirled to face him.

"My dear Phillip," she exclaimed haughtily, "just what is the meaning of this absurd behavior of yours? I have been informed that you are planning a trip. Is this true?"

Phillip smiled pleasantly. "And so I am, Mama."

Lady Delemere waved a dismissive hand. "Well, of course, that is impossible. You shall do no such thing. Have you forgotten that I am giving a dinner party for Elise's family tomorrow night?"

Phillip tapped the heel of his hand against his forehead. "Ahhh, yes, I suppose I did." He shrugged. "But what of it? Mama, you have so many dinner parties! At least one a week, I vow. In any case, I fail to see how my taking a trip would interfere with yet another one of your festive occasions."

"Do not be obtuse, Phillip," she grumbled. "You know perfectly well that Elise will attend. And she will most certainly expect your presence. Whatever could I possibly say to her that would make your absence acceptable? And by the way, just where *were* you going?"

Phillip gave her an icy smile. "I *am* going, Mama. To Cornwall. To Gull Haven. And there will be no need for you to make any excuses for my absence tomorrow night. By now I feel certain that Elise is well aware of my trip, and she will most certainly not be expecting me tomorrow night at what I am certain will be your very elegant dinner table."

Lady Delemere's complexion colored. "Phillip! You must stop this nonsense, at once! Gull Haven," she muttered nastily. "Whatever has persuaded you to nourish such a burning desire to suddenly rush off to that wretched relic? To what purpose?"

Phillip's chilly smile vanished. "I have decided to

take up residence there. Permanently. And there is no mystery as to why. I have simply grown weary of London. In truth, I have become disillusioned with the hectic and useless lifestyle that London seems to demand. I desire a more peaceful existence. And since I have not been there in years, I need to go to Gull Haven and see what needs to be done. I am sure there are quite a few preparations, and probably an equal number of repairs to be made, before my move."

"My dear Phillip! Have you completely taken leave of your senses?" His mother marched toward him, her complexion now a bright fuchsia. "Have you spoken to Elise about this…this ridiculous misadventure of yours?"

Phillip sighed heavily. "Why should I, Mama? Where I go, when I go, and how long I stay is none of Elise's business."

"But, of course, it is! She will have to live there once the two of you are married."

Phillip took hold of his mother's shoulders and firmly guided her over to a vacant seat on the sofa. He gently forced her to sit down. "You are becoming overwrought, Mama, and what I am about to tell you will undoubtedly cause you more distress. Now, I want you to take a deep breath and try to remain calm."

He took a deep breath of his own, then squared his shoulders. "The simple truth of the matter is, I have no intention of ever asking for Elise's hand in marriage. Not now. Not ever."

His mother's florid complexion paled significantly. "Wha…What? Whatever do you mean!" She snapped open her fan and began to frantically wave it in front of her face. "Oh, Phillip, do stop playing these silly games with me. Of course, the two of you are to be married. It is expected! Everyone knows the nuptials are to be announced shortly. It is only a formality."

"Then they are mistaken," Phillip replied calmly.

By now his mother's face had become white as parchment and, with her free hand, she began to nervously pat her chest where her heart was located. "Phillip, you cannot do this! You simply cannot walk out in the middle of a courtship with a lovely girl like Elise just because of some silly whim on your part. I mean—whatever will people think? Whatever will Elise think!"

"I really cannot imagine, Mama, and I simply do not care."

The fan in his mother's hand, still open, slipped from her fingers to dangle awkwardly from the cord fixed to her wrist. "But why are you doing this?" she whined. "It is...quite insensible. Listen to me, Phillip. You belong here. In London. Married to Elise. Cornwall is a wild and pagan place. You will hate it there. In a short time, you will come back here, and Elise will be married to someone else. Listen to me, Phillip," she almost shrieked, "you cannot do this. I...I simply forbid it!"

Up until now Cordelia had remained unnaturally and unusually silent. But no more. She quickly tossed aside her needlework, rose from the sofa, and hurried to her brother's side. "Well, I think it is quite wonderful," she announced forcefully. "If that is what Bepo wants, then he should do it." She tucked her arm under and around Phillip's elbow, then looked defiantly at her mother. "People should be allowed to follow their hearts, Mama, instead of always having their lives planned out for them by someone else." Turning to her brother, she smiled mischievously. "Bepo, as soon as you are settled, would you mind if I came for a visit…and perhaps brought a friend?"

Phillip inwardly cringed at the deplorable nickname she had tagged him with during her toddler years. However, it did not prevent him from noting her smile, as well as the twinkle in her eyes.

"I do believe you are acquainted with a Mr. Peter Cavanaugh, are you not?"

"Cordelia!" Lady Delemere stormed, springing from the sofa. "You will be silent! This is no concern of yours, and you are only complicating matters."

"She is doing no such thing," Phillip argued. "She is only stating her opinion, and I find I very much appreciate her support for my decision." He raised a disdainful eyebrow and finished sourly, "since it seems to be the only one I shall receive. It is of no consequence, in any case, for it does not matter what anyone else's opinion is. I have made up my mind, and so the matter is settled. As far as Elise is concerned, I do not give a whit whom she marries, as long as it is not I." He gently patted Cordelia's cheek. "And as for you, my little hoyden, of course you may come to visit me. As often as you like. And please, bring anyone you wish. Apparently, I will be in need of much company since, according to Mama, I shall be terribly lonely and will hate living in such an uncivilized place as Cornwall."

"Horace!" Lady Delemere shrieked. "Say something! Must you always just sit there mute?"

Phillip had thought there were only the three of them in the room. That was not the case. His father slowly rose from a large wingback chair facing the fireplace. His countenance had been completely hidden from view.

Looking as if he would rather be anywhere else but standing in his own library, Viscount Delemere shrugged. "Well, my dear, I really do not know what I can say. It seems the boy has made up his mind and there does not seem to be anything we can do about the matter."

When his mother began a new tirade, this time aimed at his hapless father, Phillip gently untangled himself from Cordelia's grip and quietly slipped from the room.

****

Four days later, Phillip guided his horse up the lane leading toward Gull Haven. He did not remember much about the place because he had only been there once, and he had been a small child at the time. However faint memories began to stir... He stopped his mount to study the enormous structure, which seemed to cling stubbornly to the side of a large and very steep granite cliff.

Gull Haven was made of ancient natural stone, built, he thought, back in the late 1400s as, originally, a monastery. It had witnessed many adventures since its construction, and Phillip marveled at how it had managed to survive. From the Cornish Rebellion of 1497, through several religious upheavals, to the great tsunami of 1755, the edifice had remained firmly rooted in its granite base. Even pirates had occupied the place on several occasions, and a band of Irish druids had taken possession of it at one time.

He did not tarry long, for it was late afternoon and he was bone weary. It had been a very arduous trip, and he had pushed himself and his horse to finish the last leg of the journey. After only a few minutes of studying his new home, he nudged his mount forward, hoping to retire early and sleep well in a clean, soft bed.

There was only one problem. The long, tedious trip was not the only reason for his fatigue, and he doubted an early evening in a soft bed would help. Every night since his unexpected meeting with Elise's cousin, his dreams had been filled with Bethany's image. Her face. Her hair. Those beautiful, utterly guileless eyes! And that mouth! He had lost count of the number of times he had awakened, covered with perspiration and with that terrible need for release familiar to all men. Each morning he would chide himself and insist it was only a phase and would soon pass. She was a beautiful young woman, and he was a normal, healthy man. Of course he would feel desire for her. And he felt sympathy for her as well. But soon, she would be shipped off to Ireland. She would be gone, and he would never see her again.

As he reined in his horse at the front door, a small, grizzled man, slight in frame and probably in his late fifties, came scurrying around the corner of the house.

"Afternoon, sir," he said, catching hold of the bridle on Phillip's skittish horse. "Can I be o' help to ye?"

"Yes, please. I am looking for Mr. Weddows. Is he about?"

The little man quickly removed a dilapidated hat, the brim of which was torn in several places. "I be Weddows, sir."

Phillip stepped down from his horse and held out his hand. "Mr. Weddows, I am Phillip Delemere. I am sorry to arrive without notice, but I have made a major decision concerning the estate, and I wanted to come immediately and discuss the matter with you."

"Upon my soul," Weddows exclaimed, smiling. He

shook Phillip's hand. "It be a mortal pleasure ta finally meet up with tha master o' Gull Haven. Me 'n Hetty was beginnin' ta doubt if'n you was blood an' bones a'tall." He waved a hand toward Gull Haven's front door. "Now, ye be comin' along. If'n I know my Hetty, she'll be 'avin' a nice cup o' tea for ye afore ye even ask for it. And don't ye worry a mite 'bout yer belongin's or yer horse. I be takin' care o' 'em. Ye look nigh on to done in."

As he entered the house, Phillip was pleasantly surprised to see how well the place had been maintained. The floor shone as if it had just been polished and there did not appear to be a fleck of dust anywhere. However, Phillip had noticed that the grounds, although well maintained, did need some work.

Hetty Weddows turned out to be a jolly, comfortable woman of late middle years. And if Zebadiah Weddows was small and wiry, Hetty Weddows was as round as she was tall. While her husband's face was well tanned and leathery, Hetty's looked as soft and pink as a newborn baby's. She wore her hair pulled back in the usual bun that almost all female servants preferred. But it was her smile that set her apart from every other servant he had known. It was sweet, genuine, and comforting, unlike the majority of those employed by his peers in London.

As promised, Phillip was provided a delicious cup of tea while he and Hetty waited for Zebadiah to join them. When he did, Zeb had a full, unopened bottle of whiskey tucked under his arm! Glasses were quickly provided, and a celebratory toast was enjoyed as Phillip quickly sketched out his plans to move to Gull Haven.

The remainder of the afternoon was spent with the three of them huddled around the large dining room table amid rattling teacups, whiskey glasses, scattered papers, pens, and ink. Lists had to be made, and costs had to be estimated. How many house servants would be needed? At what cost? How many outside workers? Their cost? Stock pens would need to be built...and a barn. How many cattle would be required to start a herd? Would one bull be enough? Two? How about sheep? And what about stockmen? As time went on, the costs kept mounting even as Phillip's funds slowly dwindled on paper. Still, he did not care. This was what he wanted, what he needed. It felt right!

Even as they consumed large bowls of Hetty's stew, they continued their calculations. Phillip quickly recognized how lucky he was to have secured Zeb and Hetty as caretakers. They would be invaluable in making his plan blossom into reality. Having both been born and raised within a ten-mile radius of Gull Haven, Zeb and Hetty were familiar with the working population within the vicinity. Hetty knew which girls were excellent workers and which ones were flighty and lazy. She knew their names, their families, and which girl would suitably fit each position needed within the household. The same could be said for Zebadiah. He knew which man would put in a good day's work, who drank too much, who could not be counted upon, who was honest, and who could not be trusted.

It was near midnight when they finally put aside their pens and headed for their beds. Phillip, aching with fatigue, was certain he would have no trouble falling asleep and staying asleep throughout the night.

He had been overly optimistic.

Even though his bed was spacious and comfortable, and with the sound of the sea smashing against the cliff below drifting through his open window, sleep refused to come. *She* was there. Again! Still! That blasted, beautiful, bewitching waif... Had she taken up permanent residence in his thoughts?

At some point, he glanced over at his bedside table. In the moonlight, he found the marble statue exactly where he had placed it. The image of *her* shone, as if it had a life of its own, taunting him, daring him to dismiss *her*. Growling, he rolled over, roughly dragging his pillow over his head. Hellfire! Tomorrow, he was going to put away that blasted statue where it would be truly and permanently out of sight.

She was no concern of his, he told himself sternly. Dammit, he was not responsible for her, and he certainly was no gallant knight charged with the responsibility of saving her from a life of misery. But that was what he reluctantly admitted was awaiting her. A life of misery, locked away in probably a crumbling old mansion, ruled over by a crotchety old woman, and constantly being at the mercy of four spoiled and hateful children.

After an hour or so of tossing and turning, and with Bethany's fate still on his mind, he got up and walked over to the window. He hoped several deep breaths of fresh air would clear his head enough that he could fall asleep.

The moon was so bright it looked almost like daylight outside. And the ocean? It was enchanting. Catching slashes of moonlight amid its restless swirling tide, the waves literally sparkled before swelling into large cascading whitecaps that rushed forward to crash against the cliff base. As he watched a low cloud bank forming along the watery horizon, Phillip wondered absently how many times his grandfather had stood at that very window, gazing out on a similar scene. He knew the Honorable Thomas Delemere had been happy here, and Phillip could not help but speculate as to the chances that he might also be happy at Gull Haven. Of course, he realized that his grandfather had had his beautiful, bewitching gypsy wife to fill his days with joy and his nights with immeasurable pleasure, while he, Phillip, would have no one.

Phillip jerked to attention. Beautiful and bewitching? He had used those same descriptive words while thinking of Bethany... Like a man possessed, he whirled from the window. If he did not stop thinking about her, he would surely go mad.

Earlier in the evening, as he was being shown up to his bedroom, Phillip had noticed the door ajar to a room on the first floor, just to the left of the staircase. As he passed by, curiosity caused him to glance inside. It appeared to be a very substantial library.

Since he had always been a reader... He quickly lit the lamp by his bed and, wearing nothing but a pair of men's long underwear, he headed for the library. Surely, he would have no trouble finding a book that he could focus on and become immersed in.

Upon entering, he placed his bedside lamp upon a very old but sturdy desk positioned at the far end of the room. When he turned up the wick and light slowly filled the room, a new but freshly opened bottle of whiskey appeared, placed squarely in the middle of the desk. A clean glass rested beside it. Smiling, he made a mental note to thank Zeb for his instincts. He poured himself a generous drink, then... He looked around in utter amazement.

His grandparents had apparently been prolific

readers. The spacious room was lined from ceiling to floor with bookshelves, and each shelf was full. An enormous world globe stood close to a window, and a large telescope, facing the sea, had been placed in front of a neighboring window. Several stacks of what appeared to be rolled-up charts or maps were propped up in a corner, held together with neatly tied strips of yarn.

Phillip, sipping his whiskey, began a slow walk around the room, perusing the titles of each bookshelf at eye level. He began to frown. The volumes covered every topic imaginable, but they were in no particular order. On any given shelf, there were a number of classics interspersed with books on medicine, farming, astrology. There were law books beside gardening, poetry mixed in with books on religion. Fiction mingled with textbooks pertaining to the structure of ships, while others addressed the cultures of faraway countries. He realized immediately that he would have to hire someone to do nothing but reorganize his newly acquired library. But who? Who could he find, out here in the wilds of Cornwall, who would be willing, or even capable, of taking on such a task? It would take years to catalogue and arrange the books into any kind of logical order. It would have to be someone special, someone who would have the interest, patience, and willingness to take on such a tedious job.

One particular book, slightly sticking out from the others on the next shelf over, caught his attention. He pulled out the volume and allowed the pages to fall open naturally. He groaned miserably. There, smiling up at him, was the picture of a young woman standing on a moor with the wind blowing through her hair. He slammed the book shut and read the title, *The Cornish*

Mystique.

In helpless resignation, he carefully tucked the book into the crook of his elbow, finished his drink in one large gulp, and accepted the inevitable.

Tomorrow, he would begin the long arduous journey back to London.

Chapter 5

One week later, Phillip was once again back in London, standing at the front door of Viscount Brundridge's townhouse. He had done this many times before, but today he fidgeted. He dreaded knocking on the door. What if he were too late? What if Isabelle and Elise had already shipped Bethany off to Ireland? Elise had stated that Isabelle was only waiting for a response from the woman looking for a governess. Had Elise's mother already received that missive? For all he knew, Isabelle could have received the lady's answer the day after he left for Cornwall, or any time between then and now.

He seized the knocker and firmly rapped twice on the shiny brass plate.

Bates, as expected, answered his summons. When he saw Phillip, even the imperturbable Bates was taken aback. His stoic expression never changed, but a surprised eyebrow rose abruptly. "Mr. Delemere!" He bowed slightly. "Good afternoon, sir."

Phillip knew immediately that his hasty trip to Cornwall must have given birth to gossip aplenty—if not throughout the *ton*, then certainly among the Brundridges' servants. Servants were always the first to know if anything was amiss. And given the gentle art of eavesdropping so expertly practiced by staff, servants were amazingly well informed. Judging from Bates' unaccustomed tone of voice and that errant eyebrow, Phillip surmised the rumors had apparently reached epic proportions.

He smiled faintly. If mouths were atwitter now, Phillip could well imagine what they would be like if his plan were to reach fruition. It would, at the very least, certainly cause a continuous demand for smelling salts at the apothecary.

"Good afternoon, Bates," he addressed the footman pleasantly. "Yes, Bates, it is I. I know I have no appointment, but if he is in, would you ask Viscount Brundridge if he could see his way clear to see me on such short notice? You may tell him it is rather important."

Bates immediately stepped back, allowing the door to swing open so as to allow Phillip to enter the foyer. "Certainly, sir. If you will just wait here, I will relay your request to his lordship."

Moments later, it was not Bates who appeared in the hallway but Hamilton Brundridge himself.

"Phillip, dear boy, do come in!" he called, hurrying down the corridor. "Of course I have time for you." Upon reaching Phillip, Elise's father held out a welcoming hand. "So, you are back from your adventures in Cornwall! I am delighted. Your trip was successful, I hope?"

Phillip felt like an utter cad. Hamilton, as usual, was being so kind and gracious, while he, Phillip, was about to cause the fine old gentleman a great deal of misery—in more ways than one. "Thank you, sir," he replied, shaking the offered hand. "I would not have bothered you except that, well, two rather important issues have come up that I feel must be addressed immediately."

"Please, do not apologize. There is no intrusion on your part, I assure you. In fact, you have come along at a most advantageous time. I was about to pour myself a drink." Elise's father placed his hand on Phillip's shoulder and began to guide him down the hall. "Let us take refuge in the library, have a drink or two, and discuss whatever matters have brought you here."

Reaching the library, Phillip chose a seat on the comfortable sofa and watched Hamilton Brundridge pour their drinks. The viscount handed Phillip a generous helping of port, then settled in a chair opposite the sofa.

"So. Tell me. Whatever is troubling you? Judging from the look on your face, it must be something of grave importance."

As a bracer, Phillip took a large swig from his glass, then shifted uncomfortably in his seat. "There is just no pleasant way of saying this, I fear. I only wish there were." He took in a deep breath. "Sir, the truth of the matter is, after much soul-searching, I have come to the conclusion that Elise and I simply will not suit. I assure you the fault is completely mine. I realize that I have monopolized most of her company during her coming-out year. I am also very aware that everyone within our social sphere expects us to wed, but—"

"My dear boy..." Viscount Brundridge leaned forward in his chair. "Do you not think I am more than a little aware of my daughter's faults?" He patted Phillip's knee. "And I doubt seriously if you are the one at fault. I love my daughter very much. But Elise, I fear, is very much her mother's daughter." Easing back in his chair, he too, took a generous sip from his own drink. "If you suppose this declaration of yours comes as a complete surprise to me, then you are sadly mistaken. I have been expecting it for some time. I'm only surprised it has taken you so long to reach that very wise conclusion."

Phillip let out a slow sigh of relief. "I have not spoken to Elise yet. I wanted you to know of my decision first because, well…"

Viscount Brundridge chuckled. "I surmised that, since the roof is still firmly affixed to the house. Oh, to be sure, there have been frayed nerves and tempers aplenty caused by your hasty departure to Cornwall. But this? When Elise and Isabelle hear of this news—"

"There is more, sir," Phillip quickly interrupted, "which is the main reason for my abrupt appearance on your doorstep. Indeed, it is, in my opinion, a very grave matter."

Elise's father was understandably startled. "By heaven! There is more?"

"Yes. It concerns your niece, Miss Bethany Brundridge."

"Bethany? What of her?"

"Sir, are you aware that her ladyship is arranging to have your niece shipped off to Ireland, under the guise of finding her a position of governess to *four* young children? To Ireland, for God's sake! As if it were impossible to find the wretched girl a position here, closer to home." Phillip quickly glanced around the room, as if he might find Bethany there. "She *is* still here, is she not? I mean, I am not too late, am I?"

"Young man, what are you saying? Isabelle? Are you certain of this?"

"Indeed, I am. But I have come with a solution."

Viscount Brundridge eyed Phillip warily. "Oh, I have no doubt of that. However, you must excuse me if I appear more than a bit apprehensive to hear of this solution of yours. I am sorry, but I cannot conceive of any alternative that might defuse what promises to be an inevitable explosion."

Phillip sat forward abruptly, nearly spilling what remained of his port. "Please, sir, allow me to explain. You see, lately, there have been some particular changes in my life that you have not been privy to. I should like to quickly remedy that situation without going into too great a detail. Let me begin by saying that I have decided to quit London and move to Cornwall. Several years ago, I inherited a small estate there, and I would like to develop it into a working enterprise. Well, at least enough so that it might pay for its upkeep."

He waved an agitated hand. "But that is neither here nor there. The point is, the house contains an extensive library that has fallen into disarray. Many of the books, I believe, are quite valuable, but all are placed on the shelves willy-nilly. I need someone to organize the volumes into some kind of order and catalog them. It would be a legitimate and honorable job with a fair salary. There would be free housing, and because of it, an element of safety and protection. It will take years, I am sure, to accomplish the task."

Phillip paused long enough to study his lordship's reaction. Viscount Brundridge looked rather sad. "Sir," Phillip continued gently, "I have learned that your niece is from Cornwall, and I have also discovered that she is terribly homesick. She is missing everything that she loves and is familiar with—her friends, her neighbors, her activities. Just coming to London is bad enough, but can you imagine how she would feel suddenly being uprooted from England and placed in a completely foreign environment?"

Viscount Brundridge nodded slowly. "Yes, I can well imagine. And I know she is unhappy here. A blind man could see it."

"I do not want my next comment to be taken, in any way, as a criticism, but…let's face it, sir, she is not wanted here. And apparently, she is not wanted even in England."

For the next few seconds, the two men simply stared at each other. Phillip attempted to discern what his lordship was thinking but could not do so. He could only surmise that Elise's father was weighing the merits, as well as the consequences, of each option that had been planned for his niece. Finally, Viscount Brundridge rose slowly from his chair and went to pull the bell rope.

A moment later, there was a soft knock on the door, the door swung open, and Bates stepped inside. "You rang, my lord?"

Viscount Brundridge turned. "Yes, Bates. Would you please inform my niece that her presence is required in the library?"

"Very good, my lord." Bates bowed and turned to leave, but before he could do so, he was nearly knocked down as Elise burst into the room.

"Papa?" Her gaze darted around the room until she spied Phillip. "So! It is true. You have returned!"

Rising from his seat, Phillip gave Elise a courteous bow. "Good afternoon, Miss Brundridge. Yes, I have just arrived. As a matter of fact, I—"

Elise, completely ignoring his response, focused on her father. "Papa, why was I not informed that Mr. Delemere was here? You know how worried I have been." She eyed each of them suspiciously. "Why do I have the feeling that something quite unpleasant is going on? I want to know what it is, this instant!"

"My dear daughter, I was—"

Phillip noisily cleared his throat. "Sir, if you do not mind, I think I should be the one to enlighten your daughter as to what is going on. It is, after all, only right that I should do so. And it is one of the reasons I am here, as well." He moved toward Elise. "However, I do feel our conversation should be a private one." He took Elise's arm and began to guide her toward the door. "I hope I am not being too presumptuous in asking for the use of your parlor?"

Elise's father shook his head. "Not at all, young man. And please, take all the time you need. There is no hurry."

As Phillip and Elise exited the library, the Brundridge townhouse suddenly appeared to become exceedingly small. They had just reached the middle of the hall, when, out of the corner of his eye, Phillip noticed Lady Brundridge hurrying toward them from the back of the house. At the same time, Bethany, probably because she had witnessed them leaving the library, had paused midway down the center staircase. For a fleeting moment, Phillip imagined several runaway carriages converging on one another at a busy intersection.

Elise chose that moment to attempt to free her arm from his grip. She tugged furiously. "Phillip, whatever has come over you! What is all this about?"

Phillip, wanting to avoid the inevitable collision, simply tightened his grip on her arm, whirled, and began a hurried pace in the opposite direction, toward the Brundridge parlor. "You shall know soon enough, my dear. And you shall know all of it," he muttered impatiently.

Lady Brundridge called out to them, but when neither her daughter nor Phillip acknowledged her approach, she directed her umbrage toward the library. She rapped soundly on the door but did not wait for a response. She stormed into the room. "Hamilton! Whatever is going on? And where is Mr. Delemere going with our daughter? I think you should know that I just now witnessed that rude young man handling our daughter in a most ungentlemanly manner!"

Viscount Brundridge, standing behind an imposing desk, smiled faintly. "Ahhhh, do come in, my dear. How perceptive of you to sense that your presence is required."

Her ladyship marched toward her husband. "Well? Are you just going to stand there and do nothing? I tell you, he was accosting our daughter!"

Viscount Brundridge, ignoring his wife's continuing tirade, caught sight of Bethany, who was by now hovering in the doorway. He waved her inside. "Do come in, child. There is no need for you to dawdle in the hallway."

Bethany stepped inside, clutching several books in her arms. She darted a nervous glance toward her irate aunt.

"Ivy informed me I was requested in the library, but it appears you are occupied. I can easily return at a later time."

"No, no. You are in no way intruding, my dear. Do come in." His lordship gave Bethany a gentle smile. "As a matter of fact, you are one of the reasons for this gathering, so it is only fair that you should witness the entire proceeding. That is why you were summoned."

She rushed toward him. "I...I thought, perhaps, you

had noticed these books missing from your shelves and wished to ask me about them. I am sorry. I did not mean to keep them for so long." She carefully placed the volumes on his desk. "They are undamaged, I assure you. I have taken very good care of—"

He raised a hand to stop her rushed explanation. "Please, my dear, my request for your presence has nothing to do with missing books." He waved at the two chairs positioned in front of the desk. "Do have a seat, ladies."

"I shall do no such thing!" blustered Lady Isabelle. "Not until you—"

"Sit down, Isabelle! And be silent!"

She stood, stunned for a moment, then, huffily settled herself into one of the chairs while Bethany, with much more grace, gently sank into the other.

"And now, we wait," announced his lordship.

What followed seemed like an eternity of awkward silence. Viscount Brundridge sat casually behind the large desk, absently thrumming his fingers on its shiny surface, while her ladyship and Bethany nervously fidgeted in the chairs facing him.

Occasionally, an outburst of angry voices could be faintly heard from somewhere within the house. Each time, her ladyship demanded an explanation, but each time her husband simply repeated that she remain seated and silent.

If her uncle was the picture of ease, and her aunt the image of malevolent fury, Bethany was the semblance of utter despair. If not because of the missing books, the only other reason she could think of for her summons to this gathering had to be her dismissal from the Brundridge household. She knew very well that her presence was not wanted. Indeed, in the few weeks she had been here, she had all but been locked away in her room—or so it seemed. Her only interaction with the family had been at mealtime, and even then she was rarely addressed. After dinner, it was expected that she return to her room, which she willingly did. The rest of her waking hours were spent reading, embroidering, pacing back and forth in her room, and an occasional visit to her favorite place, the rose garden. And there was one more occupation. Dreaming.

She could not stop reliving every moment of her first meeting with Phillip Delemere. The lovely night, the sweet smell of roses, the enchanting breeze which would suddenly swell into a swirling maelstrom and then...he stepped out of the shadows.

Everything about him was beyond handsome. His face, his hair, his smile, his voice, and those eyes that, when he looked at her, had nearly caused her to faint. He had softly brushed her cheek with a rose. Then...he had taken her in his arms, tangled his hand in her hair, and held her close. So close. Instinct had told her he wanted to kiss her, and oh, how she wanted him to do so. She had never been kissed by a man, at least not in the way she was certain he would. And she was all too aware of a sweet desire to experience that act. Being in his arms had caused her entire body to ache with a delicious need that was new to her, and ever since then, that need had only slightly weakened but never truly disappeared. Just seeing him now in the hallway had rekindled the need until...

The sight of Elise and Phillip together had sent a shock of reality through her. What good were her dreams and desires? They were useless and could never come true. They were simply silly distractions that would cause her nothing but misery and ultimately only magnify her loneliness. He belonged to Elise! They were to be wed, while she, the poor relation, had nothing to recommend herself. She had no fortune, no title, no position in society. She was but a penniless—and very soon homeless—vicar's daughter whose only hope for survival was severely limited. She could either enter some sort of service to her betters or, if she were lucky, perhaps end up the wife of an equally poor and humble farmer.

She was so lost in her dismal thoughts that she barely heard a soft knock on the door. The door opened and the object of all her dreams stepped into the library.

Phillip's gaze raked over the occupants seated around the desk, settling on Bethany's face. His mouth softened. "I see you have anticipated me, my lord."

Bethany's uncle smiled. "Since I have, more or less, deduced where all of this is going, I thought it would save time."

"Now, see here, Mister Delemere!" her ladyship bellowed. "I demand to know what all this tomfoolery is about. Both you and my husband are behaving like bedlamites." She glanced around. "Where is Elise? Why is she not here?" Glaring at Phillip, she muttered, "What have you done with her?"

Phillip met her glare with one of supreme poise. "I have done nothing with your daughter, your ladyship…well, at least not physically. She is, I fear, not feeling her best at the moment. She left me rather abruptly, but it is my guess that she has retired to her room."

Lady Isabelle sprang from her chair.

"Isabelle!" her husband barked, "I am growing weary of ordering you to remain seated…and silent. I am sure our daughter will not expire because of not receiving your immediate motherly ministrations. Right now, we have a rather grave matter to address and, whether you like it or not, your presence is not only required, it is demanded!" He turned back to Phillip, smiling pleasantly. "So, young man…regarding your first issue, should I assume that an understanding has been amicably reached?

Phillip colored slightly. "Well, the issue has certainly been declared and discussed, but I would be very reluctant to choose the word 'amicable' in describing the outcome."

His lordship nodded gravely. "Yes, well, that may take some time, I have no doubt." Squaring his shoulders, he cleared his throat abruptly. "Yes, well, young man, before we broach the second issue which has brought you here, I wonder if you would allow me the floor for a few more minutes? There is a small matter which I most particularly wish to clear up. It will not take long, I assure you, and it is somewhat related to your most excellent alternative."

A knowing look passed between the two men. Showing only the merest hint of a smile, Phillip bowed slightly. "Of course, sir. And as you offered me earlier, please, take all the time you need."

Chapter 6

Viscount Brundridge, pursing his lips between two fingers, slowly paced back and forth behind his desk. Stopping suddenly, he faced his wife, his expression not that of affection.

"Isabelle, my dear, it has been brought to my attention that you have been discreetly searching for a position of employment which our niece might undertake. Is this true?"

Lady Isabelle appeared startled for a moment. She quickly recovered, however. "Well, yes, Hamilton, as a matter of fact—"

"May I ask why you felt it within your right to decide upon this undertaking before first consulting me?"

Her ladyship squirmed as if her chair had become uncomfortable. "Well…really, Hamilton. I…I know you are kept quite busy managing your various investments. And then…well, you do have your social obligations—at your club and all…" She glared at him. "I simply did not wish to bother you over such a trivial matter."

His lordship, quite out of character, slammed down his hand upon his desk. "Bethany's future is *not* a trivial matter, Isabelle. She is my niece. My brother's blood flows in her veins. She is *my* responsibility, and I shall be the one to decide what is best for her. Not you. Not Elise. Is that understood?"

Bethany suddenly rose from her chair, clutching her hands and on the verge of tears. "Please! Uncle Hamilton, Aunt Isabelle... I...I do not wish to be the cause of any unpleasantness between the two of you. Indeed, not to anyone. I know my unexpected arrival has been a great inconvenience to everyone. It is, after all, right in the middle of Elise's coming out. I am an additional person that you must provide for. The servants have been burdened with additional work, and...well, if it had not been for the letter my father left, instructing me to come to you, I never would have presumed—"

"My dear Bethany," his lordship interjected, "you most certainly are *not* a burden—to the servants or to anyone else, for that matter. How could you be? We rarely see you and are not even aware of your presence in the house unless you are summoned." He motioned for her to resume her place. "Please, do sit down, child, and allow me to finish."

Bethany obeyed, almost melting into her chair.

His lordship stepped over to his wife, took her hand and placed a soft kiss on her fingers. "My dear Isabelle, during the twenty years of our marriage, I have always attempted to please you in every possible way. I am sure you will agree that any whim on your part I have happily obliged. I did so because I loved you then, and I love you now. I wanted, above all things, for you to be happy. I think you will agree that I have done the same to Elise. Is this not so?"

Her ladyship snatched her hand free. "My dear Hamilton, will you please come to the point? All this intrigue is becoming quite tiresome."

"Answer the question, Isabelle," her husband ordered firmly. "Do you, or do you not, agree with my last statement?"

"Yes, yes. Now…please do get on with it, Hamilton. I have other, more important, matters to attend to besides sitting here listening to your husbandly accolades."

His lordship, glaring at his wife, stiffened. "Well, this time, Isabelle, you had better listen, and listen closely because I have become aware of the plans you have arranged for Bethany, and I am about to overrule them."

Phillip immediately recognized where their exchange was leading. If at any time his lordship, however inadvertently, let it slip, or even implied, that he, Phillip, would in fact, be Bethany's employer, then all would be lost. Her ladyship would never allow that to happen. She would simply ship Bethany off to Ireland, post haste—and very likely in the dead of night, if necessary.

He rose from the edge of his lordship's desk where he had been resting and cleared his throat in a way that caught everyone's attention. "Uh, please excuse me, sir, but do you mind if I take over at this juncture? Since I have all the particulars…"

"What? Oh…uh…yes. Of course, my boy. By all means."

Phillip, like his lordship earlier, took several short paces back and forth before he began to speak. He had to choose his words very carefully. "Your ladyship, Miss Brundridge… As I am sure you are aware, I have just returned from a trip to Cornwall. While there, attending to some personal business, I happened to learn of a position open for a young lady of good standing. It seems that the owner of an estate there, a gentleman, also of good standing, is in great need of someone to put into order and catalog a rather extensive library that has become neglected." He stopped to give both women what he hoped was an engaging smile. "At this point, I must digress a bit so you might make sense of where my dialogue is heading." He clasped his hands behind him and resumed his back-and-forth pacing. "You see, before I left on my trip, I learned, during a short conversation with Miss Brundridge," he nodded toward Bethany, "that she is, in fact, from Cornwall. She was born there and has lived her entire life there. During that interval with her, I also surmised that she is feeling rather homesick." He stopped suddenly and faced Bethany. "Is my assumption correct, Miss Brundridge?"

Bethany paled. "Well, I… That is—"

"Do speak up, child," her uncle chimed in. "This is no time to pick and choose your words for the sake of diplomacy. For good or bad, it is imperative that you speak the truth."

Bethany fixed her eyes on the fidgeting hands in her lap. "Well, yes. Since you put it that way, I suppose I am rather homesick. But please, Uncle, that does not mean that I am not grateful for your generous acceptance of me into your household."

"Please, my dear," his lordship responded, "I assure you, your appreciation of our accepting you into our fold has never been in question."

When Bethany graced her uncle with an anemic smile, Phillip quickly resumed his discourse—before Lady Isabelle's suspicious nature could be further aroused. Already he could all but see that quick brain of hers working, analyzing, measuring every word.

"Well, now, let me see, where was I? Oh, yes, now I recall. The position of employment open for a suitable young lady. It suddenly hit me, then. What better outcome could there be, but for Miss Brundridge to assume the position in question? She is, most certainly, a young lady of good standing, and is, I suspect, well-read enough to be capable of handling such an endeavor. I was able to discern that from her correct use of the English language, pronunciation, and so on. In addition, the second time I saw her she was carrying several books in her arms." He smiled faintly. "Apparently my assumption that she is well read is correct, since I notice she has just returned to your library with another armful of books."

He stopped and allowed what he had said to soak in. His lordship was nodding with approval. Her ladyship, frowning, appeared to be in deep thought. Bethany's face was a mirror of contradictions. Phillip read worry, fear, anticipation, hope, but most of all, suppressed joy playing across her lovely features.

"It seems almost…preordained, does it not?" Phillip finished softly. "Miss Brundridge would be able to return to her beloved Cornwall. That is where she wants to be and that is where she belongs. As for the rest of you, you may continue on with your hectic lives without the worry of your niece feeling displaced." Phillip could not help but add one last inducement to seal the agreement. "And I am sure that, once she is back in her beloved Cornwall, she may never wish to leave it again."

His lordship looked quite pleased, as if he alone had been the one responsible for such a solution. "Well, I, for one, believe that is a splendid opportunity for her. And certainly it is better than her being shipped off to Ireland." He turned to his wife. "Would you not say so, Isabelle?"

"Ireland!" Bethany sprang from her chair. "*Me*? What do you mean?"

His lordship waved calming hands at his niece. "Now, now, do not become overwrought, my dear. I did not mean to upset you. I have already told Isabelle that I will not allow that to happen. And happily, Mr. Delemere here has presented a most suitable alternative to that rather ghastly prospect."

Bethany faced her aunt. "Am I to understand that you had planned to send me to Ireland? To do what, pray?"

Her ladyship squirmed yet again in her chair. "Well, really, Bethany, the way you do carry on…"

His lordship chose to answer Bethany's query. "It is my understanding the position is that of governess to four young children who have become wards of their elderly grandmother. Sounds delightful, doesn't it?"

Lady Isabelle snorted. "I assure you, my dear Bethany, the position is actually quite respectable and there are many young ladies in your…well…circumstances who would most certainly be grateful to undertake such an endeavor."

"Excellent," boomed his lordship. "Then it will not be necessary for Bethany to accept such a position. And certainly *not* in Ireland."

"Excuse me, sir," Phillip interrupted. "I believe we have forgotten something. Before we begin to celebrate Miss Brundridge's narrow escape from the dreaded shores of Ireland, should we not ask the young lady which position she would prefer? After all, she will be the one who will be performing the duties, and ultimately the one who will reap the rewards, as well as the consequences."

Bethany, clutching her hands, turned to his lordship. "Yes, *please*! Uncle, may I speak?"

"Certainly, my dear."

She turned back to Phillip. "Mr. Delemere. Do you truly feel that I am qualified for this position? You must know that I have led a very humble life. I have no formal schooling. You see, we did not have much money, so there was never any hope that I might attend a proper school. I only learned what my mother and father managed to teach me during the evening hours. That and what I have read in books. I do love to read."

Phillip smiled. "Miss Brundridge, I suspect that you know more than many learned people. And in answer to your question, yes, I do believe you are qualified. If I did not, I never would have considered you for the position."

Bethany's features, already lovely, melted into the most beautiful vision Phillip had ever seen. "If that is true, sir, then I would be most happy to accept the offer."

Phillip had not realized it, but he had been holding his breath, waiting for her answer. When it came, it felt as if a great burden had lifted from him.

His brain began to swirl. Was this the same sensation experienced by his grandfather the first time he beheld that bewitching young gypsy girl? The first time he held her in his arms? Kissed her? Was this the exhilaration he had lived with the rest of his life? If so, then Phillip knew, just like his grandfather had known, that he never wanted to feel anything else in his lifetime. And then, another truth came to him, almost as an afterthought—He had fallen in love with Bethany Brundridge, and he always would be.

He exhaled, then took in a fresh supply of oxygen before he could speak. "How soon do you think you can be ready to travel, Miss Brundridge?" he finally asked.

Again, there was that heart-melting smile. "I do not have many possessions, Mr. Delemere. I can be ready whenever it pleases you."

This was the breaking point for her ladyship. "Now, see here, Bethany—"

"Oh, do be silent, Isabelle!" This gruff and commanding instruction came from Viscount Brundridge. He stood off to the side of the room, his face glowing with approval.

Phillip, on the other hand, was within an arm's reach of Bethany. It was a temptation he could barely resist. It did not help him, imagining what it was going to be like living in the same house with her, seeing her every day, just being in the same room with her on a daily basis. Still, somehow, he managed to maintain an air of propriety.

Phillip gave Bethany a courteous bow. "In that case, Miss Brundridge, I shall return for you"—his mouth, in spite of himself, quirked in amusement—"and your few possessions, first thing in the morning. There is a coach leaving at seven a.m., and I should very much like for you to be on it."

"Bethany will do no such thing," her ladyship screeched. She started to rise from her chair, but apparently remembered her husband's constant demand that she remain seated. Glancing at him, she eased back down. "Mr. Delemere, you are far afield from being a gentleman if you are suggesting that Bethany should just leave the protection of our home without the least knowledge of where she is going. Where is the child to live? Is she to receive wages for her labors, or will she be treated as a mere chattel? These things we *must* know before we would even consider—"

"Mr. Delemere has already advised me on the particulars concerning her employment." Once again this came from Viscount Brundridge. He stepped forward until he was abreast with his wife. "Bethany is to reside within the safe confines of her employer's home, Isabelle." He raised a silencing hand even as Lady Brundridge opened her mouth. "And before you issue your very predictable concern over Bethany's reputation in doing so, you will be happy to know that I have already thought of that. I am planning on sending Grace Padmore with her. Grace is, as you very well know, getting up in years and is close to retirement. I have continued to keep her on because, sadly, she is alone in this world and therefore has no place to go. I am sure she will welcome the chance to serve as Bethany's chaperone. In any case, she has been attending to Bethany since our niece's arrival. They seem to get on well together, so I see no reason to upset a perfectly amicable arrangement."

Left with no argument to fall back on, her ladyship slumped back in her chair, silent at last, but brooding.

Phillip seized on the moment. "Well, now that the prospect of Miss Brundridge's employment has been resolved, and we are all in agreement, I think I must take my leave. I have much to do today, and time seems to be passing."

"Of course, my boy. Here, allow me to show you to the door."

"There is no need for that, sir. I can find my way. But thank you."

As Phillip quietly closed the library door and started down the hall, he breathed a tremendous sigh of relief.

He could not believe his luck. He had managed to present his case without much ado. But the thing that truly left him feeling fortunate was the fact that Lady Brundridge, probably distracted by their heated discussion, had conveniently forgotten to ask for the name of the gentleman employing her niece.

Bates, somehow anticipating Phillip's departure, was already waiting for him at the door.

Phillip accepted his hat, coat, and gloves from the indomitable servant. "Thank you, Bates," he said, smiling. "I say, it is a lovely day, is it not?"

Bates, opening the door for Phillip, bowed. "If you say so, sir."

"Oh, I do, Bates. Indeed, I do.

Chapter 7

The next morning, at a little before 6:00 a.m., Bethany paced back and forth between the window and the door to her bedchamber. Each time she reached the window, she paused long enough to lean outside in an effort to see as much of the entrance drive to her uncle's townhouse as possible. Her room was located on the third floor, and luckily near the front entrance. While it was true she had a clear view of any carriage or horseman turning into *Belle Maison*'s approach from the main road, it was also true she had only a limited view of a few yards. The corner of the house blocked the remaining approach of any newcomer. If she missed anyone turning into the drive, she would never know when, or if, anyone had arrived.

"Miss, do come in from the window. You will catch your death from all that night air."

Bethany turned and faced Grace Padmore, who was busily packing up the rest of her new charge's few possessions. "Mrs. Padmore, I am doing the right thing, am I not? I…I mean," she began her pacing again, along with wringing her hands, "what if my new employer is…is an ogre? What if he… Ohhh, I do not know what I mean." She stopped suddenly. "And what of Mr. Delemere? What if he has had a change of heart and has decided that I am not right for the task?" She let out a strangled shriek. "Mrs. Padmore…what if he does not come for us? What shall I do then? I can no longer remain here. Not after last night's unpleasantness. Where shall I go? I have no money, no friends or connections here in London. What will become of me?"

Grace tossed down one of Bethany's bedraggled chemises that she had been folding and hurried over to her new charge. Grabbing Bethany's worrying hands, she held them tightly. "Hush now, miss. You must not talk like that or even think of such a thing. Now, listen to me. The servants have been talking. Well, you know how that is, gossip and all. But they do say they think Mr. Delemere to be a fine young man. They believe he is a very honest and honorable gentlemen. Now, do you think that an honest and honorable gentleman would do such a thing? And look," she lifted her watch fob hanging around her neck and showed Bethany the time. "See? It is still much too early for Mr. Delemere to put in an appearance. Why, I should not expect him before a few more minutes, at the very least." She gave Bethany a reassuring smile. "Now, why do you not change into your day shoes and give me your slippers to pack. Otherwise, we may very well forget them."

****

At just past 6:00 a.m., Phillip, along with a rented carriage, turned onto the entrance drive to *Belle Maison*. He dismounted and approached Hamilton Brundridge's front door feeling much better than he had slept. The chance that everything could still go wrong had plagued his thoughts during the night. But this morning, even though it was exceedingly early, promised to be sun-filled and much warmer than previous days. That, he reasoned, was a good sign.

As expected, Bates opened the door. The

Brundridge's first footman was usually impeccably dressed, freshly groomed, and without a hair out of place. However, on this day, Bates appeared weary, bleary-eyed, and with his apparel in disarray. Even his vest was buttoned askew. Phillip did not find it odd to discover him so.

Servants normally took the brunt of any unpleasantness occurring within a household. It seemed that any crisis, whether big or small, could be made bearable with a fresh cup of tea replaced every fifteen minutes or so and always served with either freshly baked crumpets or tea cakes. After all, any gentlewoman knows she must keep up her strength during a time of crisis. And if that was not sufficient, there was always the option of being fanned by a servant, accompanied by a bottle of smelling salts. The last resort would, of course, be the inevitable cold compress, usually included with any or all of the above. Phillip could only speculate, with both Isabelle and Elise in residence, as to the emotional upheaval that must have transpired after his swift departure the afternoon before. However, judging from Bates' appearance, Phillip surmised it must have been neither pleasant nor of short duration.

With subdued pleasantries having been exchanged, he was given entrance. Phillip then requested that Miss Bethany Brundridge be notified of his arrival.

Bates showed no surprise as to which Miss Brundridge he was to notify. This, again, did not surprise Phillip. In addition to servants being overworked during times of crises, they were very often more aware of what was going on than the superiors whom they were attempting to mollify.

Remaining regal in spite of his appearance, Bates

bowed, turned, and headed for the staircase. Phillip's gaze momentarily followed the footman's ascent up the stairs until movement from above caught his attention. He glanced up at the second-floor landing. There, at the head of the stairs, stood Elise, watching him. As soon as he saw her, she whirled and fled out of sight. He saw no one else.

Left alone in the foyer, Phillip began a leisurely stroll back and forth within the area.

He had not returned to Delemere House since his arrival back in London. Instead, he had secured a room at his club. His reasoning was, he believed, quite sound. He simply did not want to be an unwilling participant in an endless quarrel with his mother. He did not think his parents were yet aware of his reappearance in London, and he was grateful for that. If so, Phillip was certain he would have been sought out at his club. That is the first place his father would have looked. Of course, he knew his happy anonymity would not last for long.

As he continued his journey about the room, so did his random thoughts. He must not forget to see his lawyer about drawing up his will. His tailor required a last fitting on a new set of trousers Phillip had ordered. He needed to stop by Tattersall's to pick up that list of businesses in Truro that he would be using...

He happened to pass an elegant side table situated against one wall. A silver salver on which mail or messages were placed rested upon its polished surface. Phillip noticed that several notes were still occupying the tray. This was highly unusual for that time of day because usually missives were delivered promptly upon arrival. This meant, of course, that the correspondence had been left undelivered overnight.

The Cornish Mystique

He truly was not being nosy, but he did notice a hand-delivered envelope placed on top of the others. He knew it had been hand delivered because there was only Elise's name written on the envelope and the name of the Brundridge's townhouse, *Belle Maison*, written underneath. And there was something else he noticed. The handwriting looked familiar. He stood there for a moment, trying to match a name to the cursive, but just then Bethany, hurrying down the stairs, captured his attention.

She was dressed in what Phillip assumed to be her best gown. It was blue, faded, and trimmed in white lace. Draped about her shoulders was a gray cloak, also faded. Her head was bare, displaying the riot of glorious black curls Phillip recalled so well. In truth, she had attempted to hold them at bay with a length of blue ribbon, but alas, several errant tendrils had found their escape. They teasingly floated about her face and neck, while a bonnet dangled from one arm.

A pleasant-looking older woman, bundled up in black bombazine, followed closely behind Bethany. Phillip assumed this to be Bethany's companion/chaperone, Grace Padmore, whom Hamilton had mentioned in the library the day before.

Surrounding a still attractive but aged face, a drab bonnet covered all but a few wisps of her graying hair.

Phillip felt a sudden twinge of sympathy as he studied the woman. The bonnet truly was a pathetic attempt at feminine adornment, for both its single drooping feather, and the colorless clump of flowers hovering above the brim were all well beyond repair. He immediately decided that, at the first opportunity, he would purchase the fairest bonnet he could find and present it to her. Somehow he knew she not only deserved such a gift, he was certain it would mean a great deal to her.

Phillip sensed that this woman had a story to tell, and his interest in her began to grow. There was no doubt she had been beautiful at one time. He could see that even now, for her features, though marred by age, were still fair. She should have married, had a home, been loved. Yet, for some reason, Phillip knew with a certainty that she had not experienced any of those things, save one. He would wager everything he owned that she had, at one time, loved and been loved. Yes, there was something, a veiled sadness in her features, that hinted of a story. Something tragic had happened in her life that had caused love to abandon her to a life of serving others. He wondered briefly if he would ever learn what it was.

Bethany, stepping off the stairs, hurried toward Phillip, breaking into his speculations. "Mr. Delemere, as you can see, we are ready." She blushed prettily. "I do hope we have not kept you waiting."

Phillip, smiling, offered both women a gentlemanly bow. "Good morning, ladies. No, indeed, you have not. And may I say that both of you have won my undying admiration. Just think, two women, both on time. That is most certainly a rarity."

Just then, two sleepy-eyed and hastily dressed young footmen skirted passed them, carrying a small trunk between them. Another young man, his position within the household undetermined, immediately followed, grasping a very battered case that probably held everything Mrs. Padmore owned, just as Bethany's trunk did for her.

Outside, after the luggage had been loaded onto the rented carriage Phillip had hired for the occasion, there was an awkward moment in which no one moved. Finally, Phillip spoke, breaking the silence. "Excuse me, Miss Brundridge, but is not your family going to appear and wish you well?"

Bethany glanced briefly at the house, then at Phillip, and found a sudden interest in the hem of her gown. "No, Mr. Delemere, I think not. Everything that needed to be said was voiced late last evening."

Phillip required no further explanation. He bowed again, then quickly opened the carriage door. After both ladies were safely settled inside, he gathered the reins of his mount, which had been secured at the back of the carriage, and swung into the saddle. "All right, Mr. Jenkins," he called to the carriage driver, "on to the coaching station, if you please."

Mr. Jenkins, coach whip in hand, nodded, then tapped vigorously on the rumps of the two nearest horses. The carriage lurched, jerked to a stop, then began to roll forward, gaining momentum as it progressed. Within seconds, they had cleared *Belle Maison*'s entrance drive and had turned onto the roadway, hurrying along at a smart pace toward the Goose 'n' Gander Inn.

Several blocks beyond the Brundridge townhouse, London was awakening to a new day. A handful of workers, on their way to various jobs, hurried along the dew-dampened walkways. A number of carts, pulled along by still sleepy horses and filled with various merchandise, lumbered through the streets. Phillip assumed they were on their way to deliver their contents to shops and markets that had ordered what was in the carts. On one corner, a shabbily dressed, plump woman, her age indistinguishable, was already setting up her makeshift flower stand. Across the roadway, a lamplighter perched high up on a ladder, extinguished a sputtering lamp, while below him a shopkeeper busily swept the walkway in front of his business.

Phillip paid close attention to the scene as he rode along. He had never witnessed London stirring from its slumber, and he found it fascinating. He began to wonder if he, at some point in the future, would miss all the hustle and bustle of London after all. He decided not when a shift in the soft spring breeze brought with it the distinct odor of animal droppings, human refuse and, always and forever, the aroma and inevitable soot from burning coal.

They reached the Goose 'n' Gander Inn in good time. Unfortunately, other carriages had already arrived. Four coaches were due for departure at the same time, each one journeying to a different location throughout England. This caused a rather hectic traffic jam in the coaching yard, what with so many passengers arriving at once. But Mr. Jenkins, being the expert driver that he was, managed to locate a convenient spot in which to park. Phillip helped the ladies out of their carriage and escorted them through the chaos and into the inn while Mr. Jenkins took charge of their luggage.

There was already a line forming at a side door. This was where passengers were to relinquish their tickets and be directed to the appropriate coach they were to take. Phillip quickly guided Bethany and Mrs. Padmore toward the back of the line. Once there, he reached into the inside pocket of his coat and took out several packets. He handed them to Bethany.

"These are for you, Miss Brundridge. One is for you, and the others are to be given to the persons whose names I have written on the envelopes, one on each."

Bethany accepted the packets and began to shuffle through them as Phillip continued. "The tickets I have purchased for you and Mrs. Padmore will take you to Newquay. I have included funds inside your packet which should cover any expenses the two of you might require during your journey. Once you arrive in Newquay, you will need to hire a conveyance which will take you to my estate."

Bethany gave Phillip a startled glance. "*Your* estate? But, why? I thought…well, I just assumed that I would be going directly to my new employer's estate. And excuse me, Mr. Delemere, but you have not, as yet, given me the name of my new employer. I am sorry, but I do not even know who it is that I shall be working for."

Just then, and much to Phillip's relief, there was an announcement concerning Bethany's and Mrs. Padmore's coach. Those passengers were to come forward with their tickets and prepare to board.

"I am sorry, but there is no time to explain. Just follow my instructions that I have included in your packet, and all will be well." He looked into her eyes, hoping to see excitement at the prospect of what to her must seem like a great new adventure. But more than that, he expected to see joy, because she had escaped from her aunt's devious machinations to ship her off to Ireland. However, that is not what he saw. To his utter surprise, he recognized fear, doubt, and even near panic.

What a fool he had been. What a complete idiot. Of course she would feel unease. He had not taken into consideration that she had always led a very quiet, unsophisticated sort of life, where her days were rife with routine. There had never been any unexpected changes for her to adapt to, no options to consider, no immediate decisions to make, until…her father's death. Since then, her life had been nothing but upheaval. Uncertainty. Strange, new, unfriendly people, and strange new unfriendly surroundings.

He felt a strong need to reassure her. He wanted to take her in his arms, hold her, and tell her that everything was going to be all right. But that was impossible. Not out in public, surrounded by people. And neither could he take her hand, because they were full of the packets he had just thrust upon her. He did the only reasonable thing left.

He reached out and gently stroked her cheek. "Please do not be afraid, Miss Brundridge. I give you my word. There is nothing more for you to worry about." He quickly withdrew his hand and became all business again. "It may be a week or two before I am able to join you. I have much to attend to here…arrangements to make and legal matters to work out before I will be able to retire to my estate. But rest assured, I shall join you as soon as may be. Until then, I want you to do whatever pleases you. Make yourself comfortable and just enjoy being back in your beloved Cornwall."

He drew himself up. "I have, uh, I have instructed Mrs. Weddows to welcome you and to see to your every need. She is a very nice woman, and I think you will like her very much. I am certain she will like you as well. Oh, I almost forgot. Please be sure that Zeb, Mr. Weddows, gets his packet. It is particularly important. It pertains to matters involving the estate. Just tell him… Oh, well, never mind. He will know what to do."

The line started to move, and they were obliged to move along with it, getting ever closer to what Bethany slowly realized was the point of no return.

She began to panic anew. Everything was happening too fast! There was too much to remember! She had not had time to really think about what was transpiring…

There had been a terrible row the past evening. Elise had said some terrible things to her and so had her aunt. Apparently, no proper young lady would ever even consider entering into such an arrangement as she was about to embark upon. What if she were making a terrible mistake? What if the decision she had made turned out to be insupportable? Her employer could very well be an ogre, as she had suggested to Mrs. Padmore earlier that morning. Or worse yet, he could want…*demand* certain privileges. She would be trapped there! With no money, and nowhere to go… Now that she had left her aunt and uncle in such a way, she certainly could never return to them. Suddenly, she felt lost, adrift in a sea of uncertainty.

"But, Mr. Delemere, *please*… Where is your estate? I don't know where to tell the driver to go!"

Phillip noticed the welling of tears in her eyes. He gently touched her cheek again. "Do not be alarmed, Miss Brundridge. Trust me. Everything is going to be all right."

He became aware they had reached a portly, rosy-cheeked man, and he was asking for their tickets. Phillip quickly obliged while he hurried on with his instructions. "Gull Haven is the name of my estate. You must not be concerned about its location, or worried about getting lost. It is only a short distance away from Newquay. No more than five miles or so, I should think. I am certain that whomever you hire will know of it."

They were pushed through the door by the passengers behind them clamoring to board their own coaches. "Now, once there," Phillip continued hastily, "you are to give Mrs. Weddows her packet." He pointed to one of the packets in her hand. "That one. As you can see, her name is on it. Mrs. Weddows—Hetty—and her husband, Zebadiah, are the caretakers at Gull Haven. Unfortunately, they will not be expecting you, as I had no way of knowing, while I was there, that you would, indeed, be coming."

There was no more time to explain. Mrs. Padmore and Bethany were hurriedly ushered into their coach, the door slammed shut, and a loud whistle from the driver alerted the horses that they were to begin to pull.

Phillip stood in the chaotic yard and watched as the coach bound for Cornwall rumbled out onto the road. He was about to turn and leave, when he saw Bethany's face suddenly appear out one of the coach windows. He only got a glimpse of her before the coach suddenly turned a corner and she was gone. But it was enough. He knew, without a doubt, the expression on her face, and the look in her eyes, would fill his dreams for many nights to come.

Chapter 8

"Miss Brundridge," Grace Padmore cried, "do get back into the coach."

Knowing she would not be able to get another view of the coach yard, Bethany reluctantly obliged. She had been fortunate enough to secure a window seat, but when she attempted to settle back, it became apparent her position in the coach did not guarantee her an adequate accommodation. The middle-aged woman seated next to her obviously had never missed a meal, and the same could be said for the pudgy gentleman filling out their side of the coach. And when she had leaned forward to look out the window, both the woman and the man had seized the opportunity to ease their own cramped positions. Bethany was not to be outfoxed, however. She stubbornly nudged and burrowed in until she managed to reclaim her share of space. Once that was accomplished, she concentrated on the view outside her window while attempting to calm her jangled nerves. The course of her life was changing far too quickly, and she could not quite take it all in. There had been no time to sort through the choices she had been given. She should have had time to think upon each option before her decision had been made—the advantages, and both the obvious and the unexpected pitfalls that might follow with each choice. But it had been as if she had no choice in the matter.

Her uncle wanted her to remain under his roof. But

he did not seem to realize she would always be treated as an unwelcome guest by his wife and daughter, regardless of his best efforts otherwise. Her aunt wanted to ship her off to a strange country where the family connection between them would never be noted. In that, Elise was more than pleased with her mother's notion. Only Mr. Delemere seemed not to have warmed to the arrangement and, amazingly, he had managed to supply a far more pleasant option. That was why she had so quickly agreed to his alternative. But now?

Yes, she was going back to her beloved Cornwall, but to what fate? Her new employer was a complete mystery. Was he young or old? Married, or perhaps a widower with children? Was he a kind man? A harsh, uncompromising man? Or…could he be something far worse? She knew nothing of his character. She did not even know his name!

A sudden shrill yelp startled Bethany, and her attention reverted back inside the coach.

Mrs. Padmore, having earned a window seat as well, sat across from Bethany but fared no better. Another overly plump woman was seated next to her. At the moment, the woman was attempting to restrain a very fussy, energetic toddler squirming on her lap. Beside the woman and child, an extremely handsome, regal gentleman occupied the other window seat. He sat staring out of his window, seemingly lost in thought, and completely oblivious to the cramped conditions inside the coach.

Bethany studied the gentleman's general appearance and countenance. He was dressed like a dandy, yet she suspected there was nothing dandyish about him. He was simply an exquisitely dressed gentleman.

The toddler's continued fussing failed to distract Bethany's interest in the man. But it was not his coal black hair, ice blue eyes, or profile that would rival Adonis that held her interest. There was something hypnotic about his bearing. He seemed a statue, as if not of this earth. Even as the coach bumped and swayed, he never seemed to notice, so lost was he in his thoughts.

The gentleman must have sensed her stare, for his head turned slowly, as if mechanically, until Bethany was held immobile by those frozen hypnotic eyes.

The interior of the coach had begun to warm, yet Bethany felt an unnatural chill. The man was even more handsome full faced than in profile, but there was something off-putting in his mien. His eyes moved slowly over her in such a way that Bethany felt as if she were a brood mare being inspected by a potential buyer. His gaze took in every inch of her, from head to toe, his expression completely unreadable until, just before that beautifully masculine head swiveled back to the prospect outside his window, Bethany noticed his mouth soften into the merest hint of a smile.

"I say, miss…"

Bethany, roused from her trance, glanced at Grace Padmore. She thought it had been her chaperone who had addressed her. But no. Mrs. Padmore had drifted off into a deep sleep and was snoring contentedly.

"Yew'll be beggin' ma pardon, I'm sure," continued the woman with the squirming child, "but yer've dropped them papers what was in yer lap. Yew won't be wantin' to lose 'em, I'll be thinkin'."

Bethany must have looked confused.

"There, miss." The woman pointed to Bethany's

feet. "Best get 'em afore tha wind takes 'em or they get trampled."

The packets that Phillip had given Bethany had, indeed, fallen from her lap. Now, they lay sprawled about her feet. She quickly gathered them up and, as she did so, she gave a quick glance back at the aloof young gentleman who had so captured her interest. As before, he appeared to be a million miles away, staring vacantly out the window.

****

On the fifth day after her departure from London, Bethany stepped off the overland coach for the final time. Even though it was midafternoon in Newquay, thick angry-looking clouds had begun to roll in from the sea, snuffing out what should have been bright sunlight. Accompanying the clouds, a stiff, bracing wind immediately snatched and clawed at her bonnet and cape. Mrs. Padmore, appearing at her side, took up the fight against the wind to keep possession of her much-abused bonnet and cape as well. "Oh, my dear, can you credit that we have truly arrived? 'Tis a miracle, to be sure. But what a welcome! Do you suppose we shall all be blown away?"

When Mrs. Padmore suddenly lurched sideways, Bethany quickly grabbed her arm. "My goodness, the wind is fierce, is it not? We should get inside quickly before we truly do get blown away."

"Oh, it is not the wind that is causing my unsteadiness," Mrs. Padmore declared. "It is the numbness in my limbs. Truly, I am quite certain I would not have survived another day locked up in that stuffy, bumping and bouncing, bone-breaking conveyance. And neither am I altogether convinced that my back is not indeed broken."

When Mrs. Padmore began to sway again, Bethany gripped her chaperone's arm a little more firmly. "Are you able to walk without assistance, do you think?"

"Yes, my dear, I believe so. As soon as I get my bearings. But can you? Are you not as numb as I?"

"Oh, I am fine. 'Tis you I am worried about." Bethany noticed the freshly painted sign hanging above the coaching station's doorway—The Hound's Head. She smiled brightly. "Do let us go inside, shall we? I am sure you will feel much better after a nice bracing cup of tea. We shall get something to eat, as well. I do not know about you, but I am quite famished."

Bethany had never been to Newquay. Until her trip to London, she had never been more than five or six miles from Tregony, where she had been born and where her father had happily served his parish. Curious now about her new surroundings, she paused just long enough to glance about the small community.

She had been told by a fellow passenger that Newquay was a thriving fishing village, yet she saw no evidence it was so. There were only a few structures scattered atop the cliff where the coaching station had been built. Mostly sturdy cottages, all of which were neat and well maintained. Yet she saw no evidence that Newquay was either thriving or a fishing village. Not one boat rested in drydock, nor were there any fishing nets strung out to dry. Neither traps, nor grappling hooks, nor any other fishing equipment were visible. She asked a young man handling the baggage where the harbor might be, and she was told that the harbor, as well as the community itself, was nestled at the base, and up the side of the cliff where she now stood. Bethany wanted to ask more about the community, but at that moment Mrs. Padmore moaned against the buffeting wind, so Bethany took her companion's arm once more and guided her toward the entrance to the Hound's Head.

The coaching station's interior was every bit as neat and well cared for as its exterior. A long bar filled up one end of the room. Several men had stationed themselves there, enthusiastically conversing among one another as they enjoyed their pints of ale. On the opposite wall, a large fireplace had been built to combat the often-brutal spring and winter weather so common along the Cornish coast. Even now, a comforting fire blazed happily within its depths. Tables of various sizes, complete with appropriately sized benches, filled out the rest of the area.

The establishment seemed busy yet was not overly crowded. Bethany and Mrs. Padmore quickly found a table and, before they could even settle down, a pretty young girl appeared at their table with two steaming cups of tea. After the girl had taken their order, Bethany took the opportunity to inquire about transportation to Gull Haven.

The young girl immediately smiled. "Aye, yes, miss! An' don't this be yer lucky day. Why, it be ol' Ollie Smithers ye be wantin', an' 'e be blatherin' up at tha bar jes' now. "'E'll be headin' 'ome soon, an' Gull Haven be on tha way." She nodded enthusiastically. "I be tellin' 'im about tha misses what be needin' a ride." With that, she bobbed a quick curtsy and hurried away.

"Well now, this is quite nice," Mrs. Padmore murmured as she pulled her teacup and saucer closer.

Bethany barely heard her. She had noticed three men huddled around a small table almost hidden in a dark, shadowed corner. One of them was the elegant and very aloof gentleman who had captured her attention at the beginning of their trip! But he had left the coach on their second stop when fresh horses were being harnessed. Bethany had all but forgotten about him until now. How strange that he should suddenly reappear here, in Newquay, when he had left the coach early on. Of course, she reasoned, he might have had other business to attend to in Salisbury before continuing on to Newquay. But for some reason she did not think so. Something was very odd and uncomfortable about the man, regardless of his beauty and elegance.

Their meal arrived, and while Mrs. Padmore busily helped herself to her plate of shepherd's pie, Bethany continued to study the trio conversing in the shadows. There appeared to be a disagreement of some sort. The aloof gentleman was obviously in command, in spite of his young age. Bethany judged him to be no more than five-and-twenty at most. Nevertheless, he appeared to be very much in charge and, at the moment, he was quite angry.

"You said you were hungry, miss. So why are you not eating?"

Mrs. Padmore's comment regained Bethany's attention. "What? Oh…yes. Yes, I am hungry. I suppose I was just woolgathering." She picked up her fork and took a mouthful of shepherd's pie. She had barely had time to swallow the surprisingly good fare when the door to the inn burst open. Several men hurried inside and headed straight for the men gathered at the bar.

Tension immediately filled the air. Bethany watched as the new arrivals, after speaking in hushed tones to the occupants at the bar, began spreading out into the room.

They stopped at each table occupied by a male, whether gentleman or common, spoke to them briefly, then hurried on to the next table. Instantly, the three men in the shadows rose and started for the door.

Bethany thought this was very strange behavior. Any other group, especially males, would naturally want to know what was going on. And yet? It was as if the odd group she had been studying did not want to be informed. Indeed, they seemed to be avoiding it.

As the suspicious trio approached Bethany's and Mrs. Padmore's table, the regal although still angry gentleman paused—almost in mid-step. He obviously recognized Bethany. His gaze settled on her, then his mouth softened into that secret smile he had given her in the coach.

Before, Bethany had not been able to define that smile. Now, she did. It was a strange combination of seduction, promise, and the merest hint of danger. But there was something else in his expression that left her cold. It was what some might describe as calculating, even cunning.

The group passed behind Mrs. Padmore without any further hesitation or acknowledgment. However, right behind them, a tall but very thin old man followed in their wake. He was shabbily dressed and carried a battered straw hat in his hand. He stopped at their table.

"Ye pardon, misses, but Angie do say there be ladies what be in need o' passage ta Gull Haven. Might you be the misses?"

Bethany smiled up into his humble, weathered face. "Yes, indeed, Mr...Smithers, is it?"

He nodded. "Yes-um, that be me. Ol' Ollie Smithers."

"Excuse me, Mr. Smithers, but could you tell me what is happening? I could not help noticing the men who just hurried in. They seem to be rather anxious about something."

Ollie's eyes grew wide. "Oh, yes-um, miss. That be so, sure enough. It be about little Lucy Abney. She's gone missin', she 'as. And them what come in needs 'elp in searchin' for 'er. 'Er Mam and Da be in a right dither, they be."

Bethany frowned. "Oh, dear! How old is the child?"

"Oh, Lucy not be no little mite. Lucy be fully growed. She even 'as a sweetheart. Charlie O'Malley, 'e be, an' 'e be in a fair fit 'emself, they do say." He gave Bethany a clumsy bow. "Now, if'n yew'll pardon me, miss, I be puttin' yer parcels on ma wagon and lookin' ta ma mules." He quickly dipped her another bow, picked up the women's cases, and soon headed for the door.

Several minutes later, after a hurried meal, the three were crammed onto a well-worn bench seat resting above an ancient wagon bed. The bed held several barrels, various tools used in gardening and construction, and three large burlap sacks, the contents of which were a mystery. Still, there had been enough room left over to stow Bethany's and Mrs. Padmore's meager possessions, including Bethany's trunk, and soon they were on their way.

As they lumbered out of the Hound's Head coaching yard, the first low rumble of distant thunder drifted in from the sea. But it was not the weather Bethany was concerned about. Lucy Abney filled her thoughts. Where could she be? And what was the cause of her sudden and apparently mysterious disappearance?

****

For the next couple of weeks after putting Bethany and Mrs. Padmore on the coach, Phillip was kept busy preparing for his new life in Cornwall. He knew little to nothing about raising livestock, so being the astute young man he was, he had been consulting experts. He had spoken with several owners of working estates—all of them gentlemen. A few even graciously allowed Phillip to interview their employees who actually worked with their animals. Phillip took copious notes as he learned what feed was best for cattle, for sheep, for goats. He was apprised of what signs to look for concerning livestock diseases and how to treat them. He was also advised as to the best way to protect his animals from predators, and the proper procedures to take when a sudden storm blew in from the sea.

Not to be overlooked was the brutal realization of the cost for such an undertaking. There seemed to be endless appointments with bankers, lawyers, and accountants. Legal papers had to be drawn up. Proof of ownership for the land and structure known as Gull Haven in Cornwall had to be produced. A flood of funds, or so it seemed, constantly flowed between Phillip's bank in London to one closer to his estate in Cornwall. But then, something happened to break the monotony of it all.

On his fifth day back in London, he had just stepped out of his lawyer's office on Lombard Street and was about to begin the brisk walk to his bank when he spied two familiar faces. Across the street, Adam Westcott had just stepped out of an expensive ladies' shop. And who was clinging possessively to his arm but Elise Brundridge! They stopped briefly, spoke a few words to each other, and then...Elise raised up on tiptoe and kissed Adam on the cheek! In bright daylight and on a busy public street, of all places, and for anyone and everyone to observe.

Phillip could not resist. He waited for a break in the traffic, then hurried across the street.

Adam saw him coming and waved. "Phillip! By Jove." He stuck out his hand for Phillip to shake. "I heard you were back in London. Where have you been keeping yourself?"

"Oh, I have been around," Phillip replied, shaking Adam's hand. "Quite busy, actually." Turning to Elise, he bowed respectfully. "Miss Brundridge, it is nice to see you again. You are looking lovely as ever."

Elise gave him a sugary smile, but it held no sweetness. "Thank you, Mr. Delemere. I must say, I am very surprised to see you here. Adam…" Blushing, she gave Phillip's friend a coy glance. "I mean Mr. Westcott, said someone at his club had claimed to have seen you. But of course, we took no note of it. We all thought you to be cozily closeted away in your isolated hideaway, along with your wide-eyed and ever-so-charming new employee."

Phillip realized the jig was up. No doubt Hamilton Brundridge had informed both his daughter and his wife that he, Phillip, was to be Bethany's employer. Amused, he decided to continue on with the ruse—just to observe Elise's reaction.

He raised a sardonic eyebrow. "Oh? And who might that be? As it happens, I have recently taken several new people into my employ. Perhaps you can elucidate?"

Adam, apparently knowing what was coming, tried to intervene. "Elise, my dear, I really do not…"

Elise pushed him aside as if he were of no

consequence. Stepping directly in front of Phillip, she glared up at him. "Why, Bethany, of course. Do you deny it?"

Phillip shrugged. "I am sorry, my dear, but I do not know what it is that I am supposed to deny."

Elise's eyes narrowed, her features taking on a venomous expression. For the first time since Phillip had known her, he realized she was not nearly as lovely as he had always imagined.

"Oh, you probably think you are very clever, tricking me and Mama the way you did. Well, Papa told us everything." She stomped a prettily slippered foot. "And there was no doubt that he enjoyed doing so."

"I used no trickery, Miss Brundridge."

"You lied, Mr. Delemere," she muttered angrily. "Boldly and deliberately."

"Excuse me, my dear, but I did no such thing. I simply stated the facts. Truthfully. While in Cornwall, I discovered my grandparents' library had fallen into disarray. I recognized that I needed someone to straighten out the mess, simply because I have neither the patience nor the time for such an endeavor. Hence, the notion of hiring someone to do so was born. Those, I assure you, are the facts. Furthermore, I believe I stated that the position is an honest and honorable undertaking to be performed in the home of a gentleman of good standing. That, again, is the truth. The library in question is, indeed, within the walls of my home. And I do believe, at least the last time I checked, that I am, in fact, still a gentleman of good standing."

Elise continued to glare at him. "And just what is your explanation for so conveniently choosing Bethany to fulfill that oh-so-honorable, oh-so-innocent, and oh-so-licentious undertaking? Pray, I do hope, very much, that you are not going to claim coincidence."

Phillip could not help it; he grinned roguishly. "Please be relieved, Miss Brundridge, for I have no intention of claiming coincidence. It was a very deliberate choice on my part. You see, right after learning of your unbridled and unabashed dislike for your cousin, and from your own mouth I might add, I happened to accidently meet the young lady in question." He stopped and frowned. "Oh, dear, surely accident and coincidence are not the same thing. Are they? If so, then I suppose I must rescind my earlier disclaimer. Although, either way, I still maintain that it was not planned."

Phillip thought for a fleeting moment that Elise might strike him. Apparently, so did Adam, for he quickly grabbed Elise's arm and pulled her a few steps down the walkway.

"Elise, my dear, we really must be on our way. It is long past nuncheon, and I am fairly famished." He gave Phillip a brisk bow. "Phillip, old chap, it is nice seeing you again. I regret having to rush off, but, well, good-bye for now. Perhaps the next time we meet we will have more time to chat."

Phillip returned Adam's bow. "Of course. I look forward to it."

Phillip watched amused for a few moments as Adam propelled a reluctant and quite incensed Elise down the walkway. Then he turned in the opposite direction and resumed his brisk walk toward the Bank of England.

Chapter 9

"Well, I still don't like it." Hetty Weddows turned from the stove and shook a large cooking spoon at Bethany. "Ye may be Cornwall born 'n' bred, miss, but it jes' ain't safe for a young miss ta go strollin' 'bout out on them barren moors alone. What with little Lucy Abney gone missin', an' them what looks still not been able ta find 'er, I'd think ye'd be wantin' ta stay close by. Whey, ye 'ave no way o' knowin' what manner o' heathen might be layin' in wait for a young miss such as yerself."

Hetty's comment stirred a faint memory in Bethany's brain that she had dismissed as unimportant. Now, with the mention of Lucy Abney's disappearance being brought up again, she began to wonder if maybe that had been a mistake. It was the far-off image of a man alone out on the moors. He was always there during her and Mrs. Padmore's afternoon airings, but never in the same place. Sometimes he was on foot, and sometime he was astride a big black stallion. Bethany had gotten the uncomfortable feeling that he was specifically waiting for her and Mrs. Padmore to put in an appearance, yet he never attempted to come closer or make any contact with them. Bethany did not think Mrs. Padmore had ever noticed the man. Certainly she had never mentioned his constant presence to Bethany. Since he never appeared threatening in any way, Bethany did not want to frighten

Mrs. Padmore when there was no cause. She reasoned there could be any number of justifications for the man to be out and about in open country. And none of them were sinister.

Bethany had been back in Cornwall for nearly a fortnight, and almost immediately she and Mrs. Padmore had begun a routine of taking long walks out on the moors every afternoon. They had used the need for exercise as an excuse, but in truth there was little else to occupy their time except needlework. That had become a ritual between their evening meal and bedtime. It was pleasant enough, and she and Mrs. Padmore, while either repairing or creating a project, happily chatted away while doing so. However, one could only sew so much before that became not only a chore but a monotony.

All of that had changed a few days earlier when Mrs. Padmore caught her foot upon a stair. She had taken a terrible fall, which had seriously injured her back, as well as her ankle, and she had been abed ever since.

Bethany gave Hetty a gentle smile. "You must not worry about me, Mrs. Weddows. You truly must not. I promise I will not go far, and I give you my word to keep a vigilant eye out for any heathens who might be lurking about."

"Well, I still don't like it," Hetty repeated. "Now, if Mrs. Padmore was ta be with ya, like that 'as been, it 'ould be a mite different. Them might think twice afore attackin' two o' ya."

"Mrs. Weddows, you know Mrs. Padmore has not yet recovered from her fall. She is getting up in years, as you well know, and she is still in a great deal of pain. The doctor has ordered her to stay abed, flat on her back, for at least another week."

Hetty made a rude noise, then turned back to the stove and resumed stirring a large kettle, the contents of which scented the air with delicious possibilities. "An' I'll be a worryin' if I want to," she muttered softly.

Bethany sighed. "Mrs. Weddows, if I do not get out of the house and into some fresh air and sunshine, I shall surely sicken. I have been here for nearly a fortnight, and I have simply nothing to do, nothing to occupy my mind. Why, I cannot even find a pleasant book to read because the door to the library is locked and the key has suddenly gone missing."

Hetty, with her back still turned, simply nodded. "That be so, miss. I 'spect tha master locked it afore he left ta go back to that heathen town, London, although I am sure I wouldn't know why 'e 'ud be doin' such a thing. Still, this is 'is 'ome an' 'e 'as a right ta be doin' what 'e pleases in it."

"Of course, you are right, Mrs. Weddows. I am not disputing that fact. The point is, until Mr. Delemere arrives…" Bethany studied Hetty's back for a moment. "Mrs. Weddows, are you certain Mr. Delemere said nothing in his missive to you about who my employer is to be, or even when I am to begin my work?"

Abandoning the fragrant pot bubbling on the stove, Hetty walked over to the large worktable positioned in the middle of the kitchen. She stopped directly across from Bethany. "I told ye, miss. The only thing tha master did say 'bout yew is that me an' Zeb was ta make welcome tha young miss and to be sure she's made comfortable."

"Well, there now," Bethany exclaimed. "You see? He wants me to be comfortable. It sounds very much as if he would not want me to die of boredom. Besides, I am in great need of some exercise. I am certain he would not object if—"

"If'n 'e knew about tha mischief what's goin' on out in them heathen moors, an' little Lucy still missin' an' all, 'e'd most likely want ye locked away in yer room, I be thinkin'."

The two women stared at each other for a moment. Finally, Hetty shoved a small basket resting on the table toward Bethany. "There now, be off with ye, then. But I'll be askin' tha good Lord ta be keepin' an eye on ye till I see ye back in this 'ouse."

Bethany fingered the basket. "What is this?"

Hetty shrugged. "It be nothin' but a bit o' this 'n' that. In case ye be gettin' 'ungry in yer waunderin' about."

Peeking under the cloth covering the basket, Bethany discovered a jar of what appeared to be tea, two thick slices of bread with a large slab of ham between, a generous hunk of cheese, and two hard-boiled eggs. It was enough to keep anyone well fed for several days!

Bethany laughed. "Thank you, Mrs. Weddows. I am just grateful you did not pack in anticipation of me developing the appetite of a plow horse. Otherwise, I wouldn't be able to lift the basket." When Hetty failed to respond, Bethany quickly snatched up the housekeeper's offering, and collected her shawl and bonnet hanging by the back door. "Thank you, Mrs. Weddows," she repeated as she slipped out the back door.

Within minutes she was out of sight.

The day was fair, with bright sunshine accompanied by a soft, salty breeze blowing in from the sea. Bethany took a deep breath and twirled around several times. Just being back in Cornwall again made her want to dance with joy.

For the next hour or so she explored the path etched along the cliff face. Bethany had never been this close to the sea before, and although the moors were more or less the same everywhere, she did notice a slight difference in the vegetation near the sea.

She eventually turned inland and, as she did so, she caught sight of movement off on a neighboring slope. Bethany was immediately reminded of the always present, watching man. But then her attention was diverted when a swarm of insects suddenly rose out of the sea grass surrounding her. Cawing, gulls immediately congregated overhead, no doubt taking advantage of the insects' frenzied flight. She watched, fascinated, as every now and then the birds would swoop down to feast upon the impromptu banquet. Rabbits, mice, and even a squirrel or two also scurried away from her intrusion. At times, she would stop and, smiling, watch them hurry away. It was during one of those moments when something unusual caught her eye.

What appeared to be a strip of white cloth, bloodied, appeared to be caught in the grass. It moved slightly, then quickly slipped out of sight into the tall undergrowth.

Bethany froze. It was definitely a strip of cloth, and it was definitely bloodied. Thoughts of Lucy Abney immediately came to mind. Lucy was still missing, and most of the residents of Newquay had all but given up hope that she would be found. Could it be…? Bethany hurried to catch up with the now missing strip of cloth.

Minutes passed—she had no way of knowing how many. But every time she gained sight of the bloodied cloth, it would vanish into the undergrowth. Still, she was determined to learn the mystery behind the disappearing strip of cloth, so she plunged on.

She eventually found herself on top of a low rise. The undergrowth had thinned considerably, and about halfway down the slope it turned into stubble. She could see now that the strip of cloth trailed from the back leg of a small limping fox, and the little animal was heading straight for a tiny cottage resting at the base of the slope where Bethany stood.

Bethany noted that the cottage was rather dilapidated. It was built of stone and thick wooden beams, but even at this distance she could see that several stones had come loose and had fallen to the ground. The thatched roof also was in desperate need of repair. Nevertheless, someone lived there, for a thin ribbon of smoke rose from its crumbling chimney. Bethany lifted her skirt and hurried after the fox.

She caught up to it just in time to see a beautifully fluffy tail disappear through the cottage's wide-open doorway. However, Bethany was not nearly so bold. She stopped at the entrance.

"Hello?" There was no response, so she cautiously peered inside. "Excuse me. Is anyone here?" When she still received no answer, she stepped inside.

The cottage was completely full, and yet amazingly neat and clean. Shelves lined every wall, each full of either books, or jars, or bottles of strange-looking liquid. In one corner was a small cot, and above it on the wall three pegs held several articles of clothing. Across from the cot, a small fireplace glowed due to a healthy fire dancing within its depths. A large black kettle hung above the flames.

Movement under a small worktable placed beside the fireplace caught Bethany's attention. There, curled up in a box full of straw was the little fox, and hanging out over the edge of the box was the strip of bloody cloth still attached to the fox's leg.

"'er name be Bella."

Bethany whirled around. A plump little woman stood in the doorway, her arms full of firewood. Her gray, unruly hair was wadded up in a careless bun, and she was dressed in little more than rags. Bethany could not begin to guess the woman's age, because her face, although wrinkled, looked as soft as a young girl's. And her eyes! They were a brilliant crystal blue, glowing as if a light shone behind them.

Bethany's face burned from embarrassment. "Oh, please, I hope you will excuse me. I meant no harm coming into your home without permission. I was just following the little fox, uh, I mean Bella. I was concerned about her. You see—"

"Yes, I do see." The woman shuffled into the room and dumped her armload of wood beside the fireplace before turning toward the little fox. "Bella be a bother, she be. Always inna somethin' she shouldn't, then come back needin' mendin'. This time it be 'er leg."

"What happened to her? Do you know?"

The woman pulled the box full of Bella out from under the table. "Stepped in a trap, she did. Come ta me with it still caught on 'er leg."

"Ohhhh, poor little thing! It was very lucky she happened upon you. Otherwise—"

"It weren't luck, miss. All tha animals come ta me when they be 'urt. That's why I keep ma door open. They come 'n' go as they please." She pointed upward. "Like Socrates, there."

Bethany had not noticed, but perched up on a

shadowed rafter was a very large owl, its feathers plumped, fast asleep.

Bethany watched as the woman began to gather up all that was needed to replace the bandage on Bella's leg. Now she realized what all the bottles and jars were for and what they contained. "Excuse me, but may I ask your name? I did not realize anyone lived this far out on the moors."

The woman did not look up but continued to unwrap that part of the bandage still clinging to Bella's leg. "People about call me Granny Faunus a'cause I take care o' all tha animals what be in need. I know 'bout plants an' 'erbs an' such, an' so I make poultices, an' tonics for 'em. An' I even mix up a special potion ever' now an' ag'in fo' folks 'erebouts." She shot Bethany a mischievous smile. "Whenever some'uns needs 'um. Don't come ta mind tha name I's born with."

Bethany returned the woman's smile. "Well, it is very nice to meet you, Miss, uh…I mean, Granny. My name is—"

"Oh, I know who ya be." Granny gave a vague wave in the general direction where Gull Haven would be. "Yew be tha new miss what's come ta Gull Haven. Yer name be Bethany an' you come from that den o' Satan lovers, London town."

Bethany shook her head. "No, no. Well, that is, not exactly. My name is Bethany, and while it is true that I have come here from London, my real home is, or I guess I should say was, here in Cornwall—in Tregony. I was born there, and lived there all my life, until…well, I was only recently required to journey to London." Bethany tilted her head slightly and studied Granny Faunus. "But how do you happen to know about me?"

Granny chuckled. "Servants, ma girl. I learned long ago them knows more 'n a town crier." Having finished dressing Bella's leg, she stood and gave Bethany a close inspection. "Well, them at Gull Haven do say yew be a pretty little thing and they be right 'bout that." She leaned toward Bethany as if to share a secret. "An' there be a'ready talk 'bout you an' tha new master, though most o' 'um at Gull Haven 'ave not laid a eye on 'im yet."

Bethany immediately bristled. She'd expected this might happen. A young unmarried woman, arriving and taking up residence in a bachelor's somewhat isolated country estate? Why, what else was one supposed to think? "And just what sort of talk have you heard?" she asked stiffly.

Granny, patting Bethany's arm, winked. "Well, now, miss, why don' ye do sit down. We'll be 'avin' ourselves a cup o' tea or two while we be discussin' tha matter."

****

Zeb was the first to see Phillip's approach. He had been up on the roof since early morning, supervising repairs needed on one of the chimneys. But now, Zeb's stomach kept reminding him it was past time for a bowl of whatever Hetty had been cookin' up, the aroma of which had been wafting out of the kitchen chimney for the past hour or more. He was about to step through the door leading off the roof when movement up on the road to Newquay gave him pause. He watched as a lone horseman slowly cleared a small rise, followed by a procession of conveyances. The caravan consisted of a closed coach and two large open-air wagons containing what appeared to be all manner of furniture, trunks, and such. Zeb was about to speculate as to where they might be headed, but the horseman suddenly steered his horse off the main road onto the meandering approach to Gull Haven. Realization suddenly hit Zeb, and he hurried from the roof.

Hetty, in the kitchen, stood at the large worktable slicing thick portions of freshly baked bread when Zeb burst through the back door. "Hetty! Quick, it be tha master. 'E's come 'ome, an' it looks like 'e's 'ere ta stay. 'E's brought all 'is belongin's."

Dropping the knife, Hetty turned to a newly employed scullery maid. "Quick, Annie, go find Lilly 'n' tell 'er ta see to tha master's bedroom. Tell 'er ta make sure all is well, clean 'n' fresh. I be startin' tha 'ot water. "'E'll be wantin' ta freshen up a bit after all them days travelin', I'll wager." She scowled at her husband. "Well, Zebadiah Weddows, what ye be standin' there like a stump in tha middle of a road fer? Get out to tha stable an' rouse them lay-abouts. There be horses ta see to an' trunks, cases, an' I don't know what all that'll be needin' taken care of."

His lunch quickly forgotten, Zeb turned and darted back out the door.

****

Granny, pouring hot water into her teapot, happened to glance out a window facing the sea. What she saw made her frown. "Looks like yew might be 'ere a bit, miss. There be a blow comin' in off tha sea, an' it looks like it be a mean 'un."

"Oh?" Bethany rose from the small table in the middle of the room and hurried over to the window. It was true. Dark, angry clouds had gathered not too far out over the sea. And as if to verify what Granny predicted,

Bethany watched flashes of lightning illuminating the fierce, roiling clouds. A heartbeat later, the deep rumble of thunder, like that of some great beast, reverberated in the wind. She whirled around and quickly gathered up her bonnet and shawl. The basket of food Hetty had packed for her she left sitting on the table. "I am sorry, Granny. Thank you for the offer of tea, but I cannot stay. I must hurry home before the storm hits."

"Don't be daft, child," Granny chided gently. "Yew'll not make it back ta Gull Haven a'fore tha blow 'its, an' bein' out on them moors ain't no good place ta be when a blow comes in. Ye best stay 'ere where ya be warm 'n' dry."

Bethany was already at the door, but it had slammed shut, and she was wrestling with the odd latch. "You do not understand, Granny. They will be worried about me. Very worried. I…I should not have wandered so far. I did not mean to." At last the door gave way. "If you do not mind, I would very much like to come again. When I can. Good-bye."

Granny set down the teapot she was holding and rushed to stop Bethany as fast as her aged legs would allow. She was too late. Because of the sudden and ever-increasing turbulent wind, her unexpected guest was unable to hear her shouts. Granny could only grab the cottage door and close it, all the while muttering something in Cornish.

****

Phillip sprang from a chair in the kitchen. "What do you mean, you do not know?" he thundered. "There is a storm coming. A big one! It will be here in a matter of minutes, and you say she has gone for a stroll?"

Hetty, standing beside the worktable, used her apron

to dab at the tears welling in her eyes. "Well, sir, it weren't about ta storm when she left, an' she should'a come back long ago." She looked at Phillip pleadingly. "I…I tried to stop 'er, sir. Truly, I did. An' what with little Lucy Abney missin' an' all, and thems not bein' able ta find 'er… I tried ta talk some sense into 'er, but she wouldn't listen. She jes' kept sayin' that she needed fresh air, an'…an' exercise, an' t'other nonsense."

Phillip, his face a mask of fury, his fists balled, glared at his housekeeper. "Who is this, this Lucy person? You say she is missing?" His eyes narrowed to slits and his features turned stony. "And just what does that have to do with Miss Brundridge?"

Wringing her hands now, Hetty had begun to openly cry. "Oh, sir, I be that worried 'bout 'er, I am. I…I fear somethin' terrible 'as 'appened to 'er."

Phillip exploded. "Ye gods, woman! Will you make sense? Who are you talking about? That…that Lucy girl, or Miss Brundridge?"

Zeb, having entered the house, had been standing apart from them, just inside the back door, his battered hat clutched tightly in his hands. He shuffled forward now. "If'n you pardon me, sir, I best answer for Hetty. She be blatherin' 'bout findin' yer miss, sir." He turned to look at his wife. "There, there, ol' girl. Ain't no call ta stew 'bout Lucy no more. That's why I come back to tha 'ouse. A few minutes ago, ol' Ollie Smithers stopped off 'ere on 'is way 'ome ta tell us our Lucy be found." He pulled out a handkerchief from his hip pocket and wiped his watering eyes as well. "They do say tha comin' storm caused tha sea ta give 'er up. They do say it were 'er own Da what found 'er body floatin' in tha 'arbor."

For a moment Hetty looked as if her husband was

speaking a foreign language. Then, she uttered a mournful cry, grabbed the edge of the worktable and slumped onto a stool.

Phillip ran a frustrated hand through his hair. "For the love of God, will someone please tell me what is going on? Who is this Lucy person you keep speaking of?"

Zeb turned back to Phillip. "Beggin' yer pardon, sir. Lucy be tha dau'er o' Jacob 'n' Tizzy Abney. Jacob be a fisherman 'ere in Newquay. 'E owns 'is own boat, 'e does. It be jes' o'er a fortnight ago Lucy went missin'."

Phillip quickly sobered. "Oh, my, well…I am very sorry to hear that, Mr. Weddows. I have been told drowning is not a very pleasant way to die."

Zeb shook his head adamantly. "Oh, no, beggin' yer pardon again, sir, but Lucy did not drown. No, sir. Ol' Ollie say she be done away with." He leaned close to Phillip and lowered his voice. "Ol' Ollie do say she be cut up. It be bad, sir." He looked up at Phillip, his face as white as parchment. "Sir, them do say someone took a knife an…an, cu…cut 'er 'eart out o' 'er body."

Phillip's complexion suddenly rivaled Zeb's. "Dear God," he whispered as a faint memory began to stir in his brain. He recalled his father mentioning something about a madman, somewhere over in Ireland, kidnapping young women and then killing them. It was some sort of cult, the authorities thought, but they had been unable to identify those responsible. Since the Irish authorities had been unable to locate the responsible people, was it possible that the cult had escaped over to England and continued to practice their unholy rituals?

"But there be more, sir," Zeb rushed on. "Ol' Ollie did say that jes' now there be another young miss gone missin'."

Hetty, obviously having heard her husband, suddenly came to life. It was an unearthly mixture of a half scream and a pitiful, horrid moan. "Who?" she strangled out. "Who is it this time, Zeb?"

Zeb turned to his wife. "This time it be little Alice Crumley, ol' girl." He swung back to Phillip. "Alice be tha dau'er of Mr. Crumley, tha vicar 'ere in Newquay. Them do say it were early evenin' last, when little Alice went to tha widow Jervis's cottage up near tha 'Ound's 'Ead. Yew know, sir, tha coachin' station. Tha widow Jervis be sick, ya see, an' little Alice went ta take 'er some broth. Them do say, little Alice never come 'ome, an' 'er bein' no more 'an five-'n'-ten year old. Tha 'ole town be in uproar, but them don't know what ta do! Thems be out lookin', but she be nowhere."

Phillip stood like a statue, seemingly unmoved by the information Weddows gave him. However, his mind raced. First, a young woman named Lucy had disappeared, and now had turned up murdered. Immediately following, another young female, Alice, had disappeared. Phillip didn't need to be a genius to figure out that the two tragedies were related. And it was just as clear that they had been forcibly taken. But the thing causing his heart to threaten to burst out of his chest was the possibility that Bethany might have been abducted as well. If so, then it was his fault. He had been the one who, through machination and manipulation of the truth, had managed to put her here—in harm's way. It was that prospect that spurred him into action.

He swung around on Zeb. "Weddows, get out to the stable. At once! Have me a fresh mount saddled. I've got to find her…before it is too late."

Chapter 10

Bethany could barely stay on her feet. The wind, a gale now, swirled around her, pulling her this way and that. Lightning, too, had become more fierce, edging ever closer to land, as was the rain. It now hung just offshore, like a giant gray curtain blocking out the horizon. *Granny was right*, Bethany thought miserably as she staggered on. She should have stayed at the cottage. Still, there was no help for it now, so she stubbornly gathered up her flailing skirt and plunged on. She had to get home!

At some point, there was a strong tug under her chin and her bonnet went flying away. She watched helplessly as it first dipped, then soared upward like some demented bird. Knowing she had no hope of ever retrieving what had been her favorite headgear, she plunged on until she reached the crest of yet another low rise. She expected to get her bearings there, but it was not to be. The wind had picked up so much debris that it was impossible to see where she was or which way was home. It did not help that once she lost her bonnet, her hair pins had immediately fallen out and now her hair whipped about her face, blinding her as well.

She tripped over something, fell, got up, struggled on, and fell again. She was on the verge of giving up when a miracle happened. For a few precious moments, the wind subsided. As the swirling bits of dead grass began to settle back to earth, a lone rider on horseback slowly appeared just atop the next rise. He must have noticed her, for he quickly drew up his mount. The excited animal reared, then began to gallop toward her.

The horse managed to halt beside her just as the wind resumed its fury. The rider, not wasting a moment, bent down and reached out for her. "Hurry! Take my hand."

Bethany did not have to think twice. She had no idea who the man was, for he wore a long flowing black cape and black leather gloves. His hat was pulled down low on his head, no doubt in an effort to keep the wind from taking it as had been the fate of her bonnet. She didn't care who he was. At that moment he was her savior, and that was enough for her. She grabbed his hand, and he effortlessly pulled her up behind him. She had no time to gain a firm seating before they were off at a mad gallop.

It was all she could do to hold on. His voluminous cape prevented her from purchasing a firm grip about his waist while part of it kept slapping about her face.

They continued on their wild escape for some minutes until, even though she had no idea where they were, she began to sense they were going in the wrong direction. The storm, blowing in from the sea, should have been on their right, as she recalled that Gull Haven was somewhat south from Granny's little cottage. But now, she realized the furious wind and lightning were on their left. That meant they were heading north. She wanted to question him about their destination but refrained. He seemed to be guiding their mount in a deliberate direction, as if he knew where he was going.

And then it happened. An enormous bolt of lightning cracked overhead. It startled the already excited horse, causing the beast to rear up violently. There was nothing she could do. Bethany felt herself thrown backward and then everything went black.

****

In spite of the powerful storm threatening to make landfall at any moment, Phillip had hurled himself into the saddle and forced his already excited horse into a mad gallop.

He was going by pure instinct. Although he had done a bit of surveying surrounding the area of his estate on his earlier trip to Gull Haven, he had not paid much attention to its environs. Still, he reasoned that if she had, indeed, gone on a casual stroll, she would have kept to the footpath along the cliff. However, just to be sure, he forced his mount a few yards further inland so he would have a visual prospect of both the footpath and the moors beyond.

The maneuver paid off. Before long, he noticed something unusual off in the distance. An odd-looking object had become caught in the undergrowth. Reaching it, he dismounted and wasted no time in freeing a bonnet from a spindly bush. With its ribbons firmly wrapped around his hand, he quickly remounted and urged his horse forward. At least now he knew was going in the right direction.

A few minutes later, Phillip cleared a low rise. Because of the approaching storm, he wasn't expecting to find another rider out on the moors. But there, not too far away, was a man. He had dismounted and was presently attempting to maintain control over his highly excited mount by only its reins. At the same time, he struggled to pick up a rather bulky object lying on the ground. The man's enormous black cape, whipping back and forth in the wind, did little to help his efforts, for the garment kept dragging him off balance.

Phillip, in an effort to get the stranger's attention, raised his arms overhead and waved them back and forth. "Yahoo! Hello there," he shouted. "Hold on, I am coming…"

The stranger obviously heard Phillip because he looked up. However, rather than acknowledging the offer of help, the man quickly abandoned the bundle on the ground. He rushed to his still frantic horse, grabbed a handful of its mane, and leapt onto the saddle. Before Phillip realized what was happening, horse and rider galloped away as if the devil himself was after them.

****

Bethany awakened slowly to a dull but persistent headache. She opened her eyes and recognized she was back at Gull Haven, in her own room, in her own bed. But how, and why? She could only recall bits and pieces of the immediate past. She did remember the terrible storm coming, and trying to get home before the deluge began. And there was…something else. A black-caped rider scooping her off the ground. But then…nothing.

She stirred, and there was immediate movement in the room. Slowly Lilly's pretty face appeared over her. "Saints be praised, miss. Ye be awake at last!"

Lilly was one of the upstairs maids at Gull Haven. Hetty had assigned her to the task of more or less seeing to Bethany's needs. Bethany found no hardship in the arrangement. She had immediately recognized a sweetness in Lilly, and the girl possessed an eagerness to please as well. The fact that Bethany had never been waited on put them on a kind of equal footing that allowed them to learn the process together.

"Lilly, what am I doing in bed? And, and, what time is it? How long have I been here?"

"It be late, miss. Nigh on ta midnight, it be." Lilly leaned close to Bethany, her eyes wide and questioning. "Don't ye remember anything, miss? Mrs. Weddows an' tha master feared it might be so."

Bethany clutched Lilly's hand. "D-Did you say the master? Lilly, do you mean Mr. Delemere? Is he here? Now? At Gull Haven?"

Lilly broke out in a smile. "Aye, miss. That be so. 'E come ridin' up as big as can be. It be early in tha afternoon, 'e come. An' 'e be bringin' all manner o' trunks, an' furniture an' boxes…. 'e's come ta stay, for sure! But as I was sayin', miss, tha master an Mrs. Weddows be fearin' ye might not be able ta remember anythin'. Well, yew know, what with tha bump on yer 'ead, an' all."

"What bump?" Bethany moved her head and flinched. "Ohhhh! Lilly, what happened to me?"

Lilly shook her head slowly. "I don't know, miss. All I do know is that tha master become right upset when 'e found out yew be out on them moors an' with tha blow comin' an' all. But it weren't jus' tha blow what got 'im in such a frenzy, miss. It were cause you 'adn't come home, an' 'e'd just found out that them in tha 'arbor 'ad jes found poor Lucy Abney." She started to wring her hands frantically and tears began to appear in her eyes. "Oh, miss! She be dead. Terrible murdered she was, an' now, little Alice Crumley 'as gone missin'. It was plain ta see tha master was fearin' for yew. 'E demanded a fresh horse an' went out lookin' for ye. Later 'e come thundering up to tha 'ouse, right in the middle o' that terrible blow. 'e was astride that big black beast 'e seems ta be so taken with, at least that be what Jem, the stable lad, do say. Anyway, and there yew be draped in 'is arms like yew be a wee babe. It be stormin' like tha devil's wrath an' both o' ya be soaked to tha bone. 'E brought yew up 'ere, an' me an' Mrs. Weddows stripped yew down an' put ye abed. Tha master give orders I's ta stay with yew, but as soon as ye was awake, I's to come tell 'im right away." She gave Bethany a clumsy curtsy. "Now, if'n yew'll be beggin' ma pardon, miss, I best go tell tha master. 'E might be almighty mad if'n I don't tell 'im right away." She whirled around, and with tears still in her eyes, she hurried from the room before Bethany had a chance to ask anything further.

As soon as the door clicked shut, Bethany spent a few moments trying to absorb what had happened to Lucy. Lucy Abney. Murdered. And almost immediately afterward, another young girl had disappeared. This time it was sweet little Alice Crumley who was missing. Reasoning told her it could only mean that a madman had come into the area and had begun to prey on innocent young girls. But who? And why? It was beyond her reasoning as to who could be that depraved.

Forcing her thoughts away from such a gruesome subject, she concentrated on the present. She imagined she must look a fright, so she tossed off the bedcovers and began the task of getting up. Even though her head was pounding mercilessly, she wanted to at least brush her hair and put on an appropriate robe before she met Mr. Delemere again. She frantically looked around for something to wrap herself in, but nothing had been laid out. No robe, not even slippers for her bare feet.

The room began to tilt and sway in unison with her throbbing head. Even so, she was determined not to allow Mr. Delemere to see her in such disarray. She managed to slip from the bed and headed, barefooted, for the press in search of her one and only robe.

Halfway across the room she heard faint voices coming from the hall. Male voices, two of them, and they were growing louder by the second.

"Judas," she whispered. Had the blasted man camped out in the hall? For truly, Lilly had not had time to fetch him from any place else. Realizing she had no time to hunt for her robe, she hurried back to the bed as fast as her wobbly legs would permit.

There was a soft knock on the door, and she barely had time to cover herself before the door swung open.

Two men entered the room, followed by Mrs. Weddows and Lilly. One was Mr. Delemere, looking as devastatingly handsome as she remembered him in her dreams. His loose-fitting white silk shirt had long full sleeves tightly cuffed at the wrists, with the shirttail tucked into a pair of tight-fitting black pants, the legs of which were secured inside a pair of clean and polished but well-worn boots. The shirt was unbuttoned at the throat, and a light dusting of black hair peeked out not far below his chin. Just the sight of him made it hard for her to breathe.

The other was a man of advanced years, short and round, but with an exceedingly kind face. She recognized he must be a doctor, because he carried a medical bag, and he looked like all doctors did late in the day—in great need of sleep.

Phillip strode to the bed, with the doctor taking much shorter, shuffling steps following behind. He stopped, studied her face for a moment, then brushed her cheek with the back of his hand.

The innocent gesture caused Bethany's entire body to react in a very pleasant way. It reminded her of a moonlit night, not too long ago, when he had used the petals of a rose in the same way. The recollection was so vivid, it caused a pleasant ache in her chest.

What appeared to be a smile, or it might have been relief, appeared on his face. "It is very nice to know that you have awakened at last," he murmured. "Mrs. Weddows and I were beginning to be alarmed because you were taking so long to regain consciousness. I am most grateful that our concern was for nothing."

The doctor tapped Phillip on the shoulder. "If you do not mind, Mr. Delemere, I think I should be the judge of that."

Phillip, flushing, quickly stepped aside. "Yes, of course." He turned to Bethany. "Miss Brundridge, this gentleman is Doctor Morrison. We…that is, I sent for him. I wanted to make certain you were not seriously injured."

The doctor waved a dismissive hand at Phillip. "Yes, well, now that we have all been properly introduced, we must see the back of you, young man. If you do not mind, I really should examine this delightful young lady before I verify your rather hasty prognosis of her condition. At least, I assume that is why I have been summoned at this late hour."

This time Phillip produced more than a mere flush. He bowed to the doctor. "Again, my apologies, Doctor, for both my lingering presence and my rather hasty and unprofessional opinion of Miss Brundridge's condition." He faced Bethany. "I believe I have been summarily dismissed, Miss Brundridge, so if you will excuse me…" He turned and started for the door.

Half way there he paused and turned back to Bethany. "Before I go, Miss Brundridge, would you mind telling me the name of that gentleman you were with?"

Bethany looked puzzled. "Gentleman? I am sorry, but I do not know who you mean. What gentleman?"

"I am speaking of the gentleman you were with while out on the moors. The one with the somewhat overwhelming black cape."

If Phillip had turned pink earlier, Bethany now paled. Her memory, all of it, returned in a flash. She immediately recalled the caped man quickly coming to her rescue. But there had not been time to ask his name. Everything happened too fast. The storm had been almost upon them, and she had been out of breath, as well as strength, from fighting against the terrible wind buffeting her. During the chaos, she assumed he was a stranger, a neighbor perhaps, noticing she needed help. But now? Once again that now-familiar mental vision slowly swam into focus. A strange man out on the moors, always there, and always watching them. But never close enough to be recognized. And now there was something else that she had not realized earlier. He was always dressed in black. Could the two of them be the same person?

She gave herself a stern mental shake because, while unconscious, she had dreamed it was *him*. Her knight in shining armor—Mr. Delemere. But how could she have been so silly? At the time she had not known he had returned to Cornwall. She believed he was still in London. How could she have possibly been so foolish? It was true that, by finding her gainful employment elsewhere, he had saved her from the cruelty of her unkind aunt and cousin. And yes, in doing so, he had also saved her from having to accept a dreadful existence in Ireland. It was also true that having just learned of the terrible fate suffered by Lucy Abney, and now most likely by little Alice Crumley as well, that he had naturally become concerned about her welfare. Indeed, she felt certain he would do exactly the same thing for any other young lady who might be in peril. All of his actions could be easily explained and had nothing to do with any romantic notion she may have conjured up. Knight in shining armor, indeed!

The simple fact was, while on his recent trip to Cornwall, Mr. Delemere had become aware of a gentleman of good standing who happened to be in need of someone to reorganize his library. Upon his return to London, he likewise became aware of her unpleasant aunt and cousin's plan to ship her off to Ireland and into a life of hopeless drudgery. Being a sharp-minded and thoughtful gentleman, he saw a quick solution to both problems and acted accordingly. That was all. There could be no other explanation. And certainly not one implying she was of any import to him, regardless of Lilly's claim that he had purposely rushed out into a fierce impending storm to go in search of her.

No, the idea of him caring enough for her to risk his well-being in a vicious storm was beyond reason. He was simply a conscientious gentleman who would have done the same thing for anyone.

She frowned. So then begs the question.... If Mr. Delemere was the man who brought her back to Gull Haven, who was the man who had initially attempted to rescue her?

"Miss Brundridge? Is there some reason you are not

willing to name the gentleman in question?"

"What? Oh, no…no, of course not. In truth, sir, I have no idea who the gentleman was. He just happened upon me struggling to get home before the storm broke. He plucked me off the ground and was heading for some semblance of shelter. At least, I assumed that was his destination. Then, a vicious bolt of lightning startled his horse. It suddenly reared up and I was tossed to the ground. I guess I hit my head, because I do not recall anything after that. Well, that is, not until I woke up and discovered I was safely back at Gull Haven."

Phillip studied her face, looking for any sign of deception. He found none, even though her response seemed to border on the ridiculous. If that had been the case, why would the gentleman have suddenly left her unconscious and lying in a heap out on the desolate moors with a terrible storm looming over them? And yet…? Her expression was completely guileless, and those heart-melting eyes of hers still held that complete innocence Phillip remembered so well. So was she telling him the truth, or had she met someone during the time he had been kept in London and she was just reluctant to say so? She might think that, because she had met a promising suitor, it might somehow put her position of employment in jeopardy. In the past, many a young maiden had run away in the middle of the night with some carefree young man, while leaving her employer without so much as a notice. Phillip wanted very much to believe her, but could he? He had come to hate deception. Elise, and those of her ilk, had taught him that lesson all too well.

When his conscience suddenly reminded him that he was guilty of that very same offense, he almost flinched.

And even though he used altruistic intent in his defense, he knew the better of it. It was with great relish that he knowingly and willingly deceived all of them. He had deceived Elise, her father and mother, and had, to some degree, been deceiving his own parents by not confessing to them his sudden and unrelenting desire for a most unsuitable young miss. Not for Elise or for any other young lady within their social status. No, no. He needed to admit to himself, as well as to them, that he had fallen in love with a poor, homeless, and quite improbable young lady. A vicar's daughter, for God's sake! But before he admitted his deception to his peers, it was of utmost importance that he confess his most appalling deception to Bethany—that he was, in fact, the gentleman whose library she had been engaged to organize. He dreaded doing so, because he knew for a certainty she would not have accepted such a position if she had known who her true employer would be. He was certain because of his connection and past history with her hateful cousin.

He finally gave her a curt nod, then briskly strode from the room, shutting the door behind him with more force than was necessary.

Chapter 11

Bethany woke the next morning with only a slight headache. Doctor Morrison had said she would probably have some discomfort for a few days, but he had also assured her there was nothing to worry about.

Lilly arrived almost immediately with a morning tray of hot chocolate and a scone, the scone already buttered and covered with clotted cream. "Mornin', miss." She placed the tray on a side table next to a window, then, humming a gay song, she began to fling open the draperies.

As the sunshine flooded into the room, Bethany realized it must be late. She tossed the covers aside and began getting up. "Good morning to you, Lilly. You seem awfully happy this morning. I am sure you did not get much rest, not with you looking after me for most of the night."

"Oh, don't ye be botherin' 'bout me, miss. I feel fine an' tis a lovely mornin'." Turning, Lilly studied Bethany. "Ye certain ye be well enough ta be up an' around? "If'n not, tha master do say for ye ta stay abed."

"Just like you, Lilly, I feel fine."

"Well, if'n ye do be okay, then tha master do say 'e wants ta see ye as soon as may be."

Bethany's heart jerked. So...it had not been just wishful thinking after all. Mr. Delemere had, indeed, arrived to take up permanent residence at his new home in Cornwall. She had wondered if perhaps she had dreamed it. But then she recalled how he had sent for a doctor, how he had stood beside her bed, and how he had gently touched her cheek, his expression showing such relief. And now he appeared to be eager to see her.

Giving herself a mental shake, she forced her thoughts away from any reckless woolgathering. She needed to be careful and not allow her imagination to read anything more into it. After yesterday's fray, Mr. Delemere was probably quite ready to hand her off to her new employer. And that could possibly be today. Why else would he be so anxious to see her? Indeed, he must be more than eager to be rid of the tiresome little waif who seemed to always cause chaos wherever she went.

She slipped into her robe and headed for the breakfast tray Lilly had left her.

She supposed she couldn't blame him. She had first created a great upheaval in her uncle's home, just by appearing on his doorstep. Then there was the terrible tension between her and her cousin. He had witnessed that in the library on the day he had called and found Elise not at home. Next came the apparent very unpleasant termination of Mr. Delemere and Elise's romantic association. But surely, no one could possibly lay that fiasco at her feet. Or…could they? Somehow Elise had found out about her cousin meeting her suitor in the garden on the night of the Brundridge's musicale. That, combined with the very private meeting between them in the library would be more than enough to cast her as the impetus for their breakup. Even her flight back to Cornwall, with the help of Mr. Delemere, had been contentious in the extreme, and it had caused him a great deal of aggravation, she was sure. But this last indictment, when he felt obliged to go out in a terrible storm to collect her when, by rights, she should have been safely home… Well, that surely must be the last straw.

After partaking of what was provided on her breakfast tray, she took great care with her toilette, then started downstairs. Just in case she was to meet her new employer that day, she had chosen to wear her best dress, the faded blue one with the bedraggled lace still clinging to the scooped neck and cuffs. Her hair proved hopeless. She spent some minutes attempting any sort of semblance of a hairstyle, but to no avail. She had finally given up and used a length of ribbon to contain the curls at the back of her neck. That also proved impossible, for several stubborn tendrils had already begun to escape the ribbon's clutches as she stepped off the bottom stair.

She should have been happy and excited at the thought of meeting her new employer and beginning her new life. Instead, she felt as if she were heading to prison with an unknown but probably very unpleasant existence.

As she entered the dining room in search of a more substantial breakfast than the one Lilly had presented, she paused in the doorway. Mr. Delemere was still seated at the table. His plate had been shoved aside and a group of scattered papers had taken its place. He held one of them, studying whatever information had been written there while he chewed on the end of a pen. Apparently, judging from the expression on his face, the information was not pleasing.

He must have sensed her presence, for he looked up, immediately rose, and gave her a small bow. "Miss Brundridge. Good morning. Are you certain you are well enough to be up and about?"

Bethany returned his bow with a small curtsy. "Good morning, sir. Yes, I am well. Thank you."

He gave a lazy wave toward the sideboard. "Please, do help yourself. It appears Mrs. Weddows has found us an exceptional cook, and I am aware that you missed yesterday's evening meal. You must be starved. Everything should still be warm, I think, since it has not been laid out very long."

Bethany hadn't realized just how hungry she truly was until he mentioned it. She made her way to the sideboard and filled her plate with eggs, seasoned potatoes, and a generous slab of ham. She passed over the beans, kippers, and sausages. She was not fond of kippers, and the sausages, as well as the beans, were nearly always available. She finished off her fare with some fresh strawberries, topped off with more clotted cream, and a delicious-looking scone.

She turned, expecting to join her benefactor at the table, but found him still standing. He had gathered up his papers, as well as his pen and the inkwell.

"Please take your time having breakfast, Miss Brundridge. There is no hurry, but when you have finished, I would like to have a word with you—in private. I will be in the salon." His expression turned grave as he added, "It appears we have much to talk about, so we might as well get on with it." He started to leave, stopped, and turned back to her. "If you do not mind, would you please tell Dolly that I should very much like more coffee. As I have said, I will be in the salon." He gave her a stiff nod, then quickly strode from the room.

Bethany stood for a moment, plate in hand, staring

at the empty doorway. Something was amiss! She could feel it, and she recognized it in his manner.

We might as well get on with it, he had said.

She hurried to the table to put down her plate before she dropped it. Her first horrible thought was that somehow, for some reason, her offer of employment must have been withdrawn. She was certain that had to be it because there had been no time for anything else to have occurred.

She gripped the table in an effort to steady herself. What was she to do if that were true? Where could she go? For all intents and purposes, she was now alone in the world. Her Aunt Isabelle would certainly see that no recommendation would be forthcoming from that quarter. Not after that horrendous confrontation in Uncle Hamilton's library, and then her abrupt departure from their home, and in the company of Mr. Delemere, a bachelor with a past romantic attachment to their daughter. No, that was a closed book never to be reopened. So…with no references, how could she possibly apply for any position at all and expect to be considered?

Having completely lost her appetite, Bethany left her breakfast untouched and went in search of Dolly.

A few minutes later, she stood at the door leading into the salon. She knocked softly and, after a brief pause, her request to enter was answered.

Mr. Delemere sat at a small writing desk by a sunlit window, writing on one of the papers he'd had in the dining room. After a moment, but what seemed like ages to her, he put down his pen, rose, and went to a small chair situated in a corner. He placed it beside the writing desk.

"Please, do sit down, Miss Brundridge."

She was surprised her legs would carry her, but she managed to reach the chair and sank down onto its cushioned seat.

Mr. Delemere resumed his seat. But then, instead of getting on with the interview, his expression turned stony. His brows furrowed, his mouth grim. An awkward silence followed. It was as if he were in deep thought as he stared, unblinking, down at his paperwork.

Moments passed. Bethany squirmed in her chair, but Mr. Delemere remained perfectly rigid, except for the flexing muscle in his jaw. She realized, then, that he was gritting his teeth and her heart sank. *He is trying to find the words to tell me that I no longer have employment here in Cornwall.*

She opened her mouth to speak when he suddenly leaned back in his chair and looked at her. "Have you been happy here, Miss Brundridge?"

Startled, she was not expecting that to be the topic of their conversation. "What? Oh, uh…yes. Yes, sir. I have, but—"

"And do you like Mr. and Mrs. Weddows?"

"Yes, of course. Very much, but—"

"I am very pleased to hear it because they certainly have become very fond of you. Quite so, as a matter of fact."

She smiled softly. "That is nice to hear. Thank you for telling—"

"How about the servants, Miss Brundridge? Dolly? Lilly? And the others? I have not had time to learn all of their names, but I am sure I will shortly. How about them? Do you like them as well?"

Bethany leaned forward in her chair. "Mr.

Delemere, please! What is all this about? When you said we needed to have a private discussion, I assumed the subject would be particulars relating to my employment, not how well I have been getting along with the staff here at Gull Haven. Now, I do wish you would come to the point. You seem to be loath to do so, and I am beginning to wonder if the offer of employment which I accepted has been withdrawn. If that is the case, then please say so."

Another long moment of awkward silence followed. Bethany, once again, squirmed in her chair while Phillip, in turn, stared at her angrily.

After a few more strained moments, he rose suddenly from his chair, grabbed her hand, and dragged her to her feet.

"Come, Miss Brundridge. There is something I must show you, as well as something you must see," and he began to pull her across the room and out into the hall.

Halfway down the corridor, he stopped, took a key from his pocket, unlocked a door, and pushed it open. Stepping aside, he gave her a stiff nod, then made a sweeping gesture with his hand toward the room. "There, Miss Brundridge, do have a look."

Bewildered, and yet curious, Bethany cautiously stepped into the room.

She could see very little, for the room was quite dark. Thick drapes had been tightly drawn across a bank of windows. She did sense that the room was large, but its stagnant, musty air indicated that it had not been in use for a long while.

Phillip brushed past her. "Just a moment. Let me light a lamp for you."

Bethany didn't realize where they were until,

moments later, the interior began to appear.

She caught her breath, unable to take it all in as the shadows began to recede, and the room bloomed to life. They were in the library that had been locked since her arrival at Gull Haven.

Never had she seen anything comparable. The high-ceilinged room was enormous. A giant fireplace, empty and cold, dominated one wall, while a huge desk sat situated in the middle of the room. Placed in front of the desk were two comfortable-looking, overstuffed chairs. A few feet away, two small sofas rested across from each other with a low table in between. But aside from the row of heavily draped windows, and the enormous fireplace, every wall was lined from ceiling to floor with shelves filled with books. In one corner, a stack of what appeared to be rolled-up maps leaned against one of the lower bookshelves. Across from them, an exceptionally large world globe took up more space. A few feet further along, a spyglass rested with its lens tilted toward the floor.

"Oh, my," she sighed, wandering further into the room.

"There, now you see, Miss Brundridge?" Phillip barked, shutting the door firmly. He drew himself up, as if bracing for some unknown, but certain, form of contention. "It is time I confessed to a ruse I have played upon you, your family, and my own family as well. In case you have not already surmised, I am the gentleman in good standing, the gentleman in need of someone to organize and catalog his library." He took several strides toward her until he stood directly in front of her. "And it is I," he finished softly, "who happen to be your new employer."

Bethany had no time to speak for, suddenly, a commotion erupted from down the hall by way of pounding on the front door. A loud bang followed as the door, apparently having been thrown open, hit the wall.

Then…"Phillip, my dearest, where are you?" came a shrill female voice followed by the sound of hurried footsteps. "Do come and welcome your guests. We have arrived to offer you moral support."

"What the devil…?" Phillip hurried to the library door and yanked it open.

Cordelia, his sister, stood there, her hand held ready to knock on the door he had just flung open. "Ahhh, there you are, Bepo." She darted a glance over Phillip's shoulder. "And unless I miss my guess, that extremely attractive young lady behind you must be your very charming new librarian." Smiling she winked at Phillip. "How delightful," she cooed softly. "Well done, brother dear."

Just then, a handsome young man whom Phillip recognized as Peter Cavanaugh appeared behind Cordelia, panting from exertion. Peter held an enormous valise which he immediately allowed to drop to the floor. Reaching around Cordelia, he offered his hand to shake.

"Phillip, old boy, I do hope you will allow me to apologize for this rather unexpected intrusion upon your privacy. I tried to tell Cordelia that we should write you first and wait for an invitation. But you know your sister. Once she gets a notion into her head, there is no stopping her."

Phillip, accepting Peter's hand, shook it firmly. "Peter! It is nice to see you again, even if it is somewhat of a surprise." He turned a disapproving glare on his sister. "Cordelia. And may I ask, just what are you doing here?"

Cordelia brushed past her brother as if he were not there. "Well, Bepo, you did say that I could visit you anytime I liked." She glanced back over her shoulder and smiled coyly at Phillip. "And you did say I could bring a guest." Turning back, she continued her stroll toward Bethany, until she reached her. She stopped, her smile broadening. "And you, I presume, are Bepo's new employee. Miss Bethany Brundridge, I believe?" She gave Bethany a perky curtsy.

Phillip, forgetting Peter was there, hurried after his sister. "Cordelia, for heaven's sake, will you *please* stop calling me by that wretched nickname. And while you are at it, will you please behave yourself."

"Why, Be…I mean, Phillip, dear, whatever do you mean? I thought I was behaving quite properly. All I have done was introduce myself to Miss Brundridge. And I was on the verge of telling her how much it pleases me for you to have such a charming new employee."

"That is not what I mean, and you bloody well know it. Now, I want to know why, at this particular time, you have a sudden desire to come for a visit. You, by any chance, would not have been sent here by Mama to spy on me and…and that is another thing! Just how did you know Miss Brundridge's name, or that I have employed her?"

Bethany, standing beside brother and sister, had become paralyzed from all that was happening, and the fact that it was happening all at once, was too much to take in. She didn't know what to do—stay or flee—laugh or cry.

Cordelia waved a limp hand at Phillip. "Oh brother, my dearest, you really are quite dull headed. Of course,

I know about Miss Brundridge! Between Mama spending hour upon hour ranting over your very peculiar behavior, and Lady Isabelle wearing out the cobblestones between their home and ours, I have learned quite a lot about Miss Brundridge. It is a proven fact that both aforementioned ladies have already gone through several bottles of smelling salts since you quit London for the wilds of Cornwall. And poor Father! He has taken to his club and refuses to come home." Cordelia shrugged, then grinned. "Why, everyone in London knows about Miss Brundridge. One cannot go anywhere without hearing her name brought up. And I think it is quite delicious."

"Cordelia!" Phillip thundered. "That is most unkind. You ought to be ashamed of yourself. Now, you will apologize to Miss Brundridge at once."

Cordelia looked honestly astounded. "But why, Bepo?" She darted a glance first at Bethany and then at her brother. "If anything, I have just given her a great compliment. It is wonderful, and I must admit that I am quite envious of Miss Brundridge. I only wish I could be the subject of such excitement."

"Cordelia, I truly do believe that you have taken leave of your senses," Phillip muttered.

"On the contrary. This is 1865, Phillip. It is high time that these archaic rules of what is correct and what is not are forever abolished. It is time for women to be allowed to think for themselves and make their own choices—without some man telling them what they are allowed to do and not do. Women should have the right to go where they wish, think what they will, and behave as they may. Why, we cannot even speak to a man unless we have been *properly* introduced. And this scandalous business about being alone in a room with a man who is not their father, or husband, or brother, is absurd."

Phillip opened his mouth to speak, but Cordelia stopped him. "I know what everyone is so afraid will happen. But it never occurs to them that the roles could very well be reversed."

Mr. Cavanaugh had quietly followed them further into the library but had remained silent and had kept his distance. Cordelia, without further ado, defiantly walked over to him and, before the gentleman realized what was going to happen, she placed her hands on either side of his head and kissed him firmly on the mouth.

She released him and stepped back. Peter immediately turned a bright scarlet and became quite nervous.

"There, dear brother. I have kissed a young man and the world did not come to an end. I did not have to wait until he wanted to kiss me, or until we were married. I wanted to kiss him now, and so I did. Does that make me a bad person? I think not."

By then, Mr. Cavanaugh looked as if he might pass out. "Mi…Mi…Mister Delemere. Please! I assure you, I—"

Phillip waved a dismissing hand at Peter. "There is no need to explain, or apologize, Cavanaugh. Believe me, by now I am well aware of my sister's unbridled behavior."

Phillip didn't have time to respond further because there was a soft knock on the door.

"What the devil…" he muttered. Then he shouted, "Enter!"

Dolly stepped into the room and gave Phillip a clumsy curtsy. "'opin' ye be excusin' me, sir, but Miz

Weddows be wonderin'.... Since ye be 'avin' guests, ye might be wantin' a tea tray instead o' the coffee."

Phillip wiped his brow hastily. "Thank you, Dolly. Please tell Mrs. Weddows that will be fine."

Dolly bobbed another curtsy and turned to leave.

"Oh, and Dolly, please tell Mrs. Weddows to turn out..." Phillip looked at Cordelia. "Is there anyone else with you?"

"Just Annie, my maid," she replied sweetly.

"How about the coachmen?"

"There is only one, and arrangements were made in Newquay for his lodgings."

Phillip turned his attention back to Dolly. "Two more bedrooms, then, Dolly. And there will be one more guest in the servant's quarters."

A short time later, tea arrived and while Cordelia and Bethany sipped their teacups, Phillip and Peter had much stronger fare. There was still more than half a bottle left of the whiskey Zeb had so thoughtfully left Phillip in the library, and Phillip intended to drink every drop of it.

He had just finished refilling his and Peter's glass, when there was yet another commotion emanating from the hallway.

"Ye gods," Phillip bellowed. "What in heaven's name is happening now? I thought Cornwall was a quiet, peaceful pla—"

The library door suddenly burst open and there, standing in the doorway, was his mother, the Lady Eugenie. Right behind her, Elise's mother the Lady Isabelle stood fanning herself furiously. And behind her, Elise stood, dabbing at her eyes with a delicate, lace-trimmed handkerchief. All three marched into the room in unison like a well-trained army approaching an enemy.

Lady Delemere shook a furious finger at her son. "Now, see here, Phillip. I have had just about enough of your foolishness. You will return to London immediately and start behaving like the gentleman your breeding demands. Elise has been gracious enough to forgive your slight indiscretion, which I am certain has been brought on by a moment of insanity." Her face soured. "I've no doubt you inherited *that* trait from that uncouth grandfather of yours." She then whirled around and marched over to where Bethany sat beside Cordelia on one of the small sofas.

Cordelia, anticipating her mother's intention, quickly grabbed one of Bethany's hands and squeezed it gently.

"And *you*, young woman, will leave this house immediately. Within the hour."

Bethany attempted to rise, but having anticipated her mother's intention, Cordelia was not about to let that happen. Still holding Bethany's hand firmly, she prevented Bethany from any change in position.

Brother and sister then made eye contact. A message passed between them. That is when Phillip slowly and carefully placed his half-empty glass of whiskey on the desk and walked over to his mother with purpose in every step.

"Mama, I do believe you have overstepped yourself. You seem to have forgotten where you are, who you are speaking to, and what you are saying. So allow me to clarify your error. This is *my* house, *my* home, and I am a grown man—independent of your edits and whims. *I* rule this house. Not you. And I will determine who is welcome here and who is not."

Lady Delemere's face turned a frightening shade of puce. "Now, see here, Phillip, I—"

"No, Mama, *you* see here! I love you, Mama, as much as any son could love his mother. But you are no longer the arbiter of my every move, my every thought." He looked around, then back to his mother. "Every person in this room is my guest and is welcome here. And that includes you, Mama. But I strongly suggest, and fervently hope, that you will not cause me to withdraw my welcome in your case."

A mournful sob suddenly sounded from Elise. She stood a short distance away, delicately dabbing at her eyes as one sob followed another.

Phillip marched over to the bell rope and gave it a furious yank. "I do hope tears are accompanying your caterwauling this time, my dear, for those feminine wiles of yours no longer hold any sway with me."

Dolly reappeared shortly, this time breathless from exertion. "You rang, sir?"

"Yes, Dolly. It seems I must revise my earlier orders. Please tell Mrs. Weddows to turn out every bedroom in the place. As soon as possible. Also, tell Cook she will need to add plenty of water to the soup, for there will be a full table for dinner tonight!"

Chapter 12

As soon as the door closed behind Dolly, a terrible row began in the library, with everyone verbally chastising each other.

Viscountess Delemere was apparently angry with everyone, and she made certain that everyone knew it. She was especially incensed with her son for walking away from his position in society and therefore refusing to live up to his obligation to his family. But his ultimate crime, in her eyes, had been his shabby treatment of Elise by refusing to marry her, and then, compounding that unforgivable *faux pas*, he had run off with a tawdry little vicar's daughter.

Lady Isabelle had her say as well. Marching over to Bethany, she stood in front of her niece and openly accused her of being a tart, claiming she had knowingly seduced and maliciously lured Mr. Delemere away from her daughter.

Bethany could stand no more humiliation. When Lady Isabelle became distracted by someone else's incriminations, and turned to join in the tirade, Bethany somehow managed to free her hand from Cordelia's iron grip. She hurried from the room and, not waiting to fetch either bonnet or shawl, fled from the house.

She hadn't any destination in mind when she burst from the back door. She only knew she had to get away from Gull Haven and all the turmoil and unhappiness there. But most of all, she needed to flee from the realization of Mr. Delemere's confession.

Unfortunately, her flight was not achieving that. The fact that Mr. Delemere was her new employer kept repeating itself over and over in her head. Her employer was not some stranger she had, as yet, to meet. Someone, anyone, who might have kept her occupied enough so that her silly longing to experience Mr. Delemere's touch, the sensation of his embrace, his mouth touching hers, might slowly fade away. And that is the way it must be!

On several occasions, before she had departed from *Belle Maison*, and when her cousin had managed to catch her alone, Elise had arrogantly stated that she had no intention of giving up her quest to marry Mr. Delemere. Why should she? She claimed Bethany was, at most, merely an expression of charity by Mr. Delemere. And that is where his interest in her ended. The mere idea that Bethany might be hoping for anything more, and certainly anything of a romantic nature, was completely ludicrous! A gentleman of the peerage? Developing romantic feelings for an ignorant little vicar's daughter? Why, that was absurd as well as pathetic! Lascivious, lewd, even lustful inclinations, perhaps. Men were like that. But Mr. Delemere certainly had nothing honorable in mind.

As Bethany stumbled along, all of Elise's ugly words and accusations mingled with the implications and repercussions of Mr. Delemere's declaration. Now she understood the reason and true depth of Lady Delemere's ire, as well as her aunt and cousin's cruel and hate-laced accusations. They had good reason for feeling as they did!

She needed time to think, to make plans, and to gain control over her vacillating emotions. She felt fury, then sadness, followed by fear, and ultimately an almost crippling loneliness that she had never felt before. Fury that Mr. Delemere had deliberately deceived her and thereby put her into an impossible position. Sadness because she realized she must leave at once, and that what she had hoped would be a sound and pleasant future had only been an illusion. That fact brought on the fear. What was she to do? Where was she to go? She had no money, and no references in which to gain respectable employment. What was to become of her? Crippling loneliness quickly followed as she realized she was completely alone now. Just a few hours ago she had enjoyed the warmth and acceptance of Zeb and Hetty, of Dolly and Lilly and the rest of the servants at Gull Haven. Now, she would have to leave them behind as well, and go…where?

Without warning, a new impediment arose. What was she to do about Mrs. Padmore? Her friend, companion, and chaperone was still very much abed with what Dr. Morrison now strongly suspected might be a fractured spine. If that were the case, then what was to become of her if Bethany were to walk away?

She hadn't been aware she was heading for Granny Faunus's cottage until she looked up and saw the little hut nestled at the bottom of the slope where she stood. Apparently, her subconscious knew she would find at least a semblance of peace there among the many jars of potions and the several cots of injured animals. And there would be Granny with her sweet face, gentle manner and, Bethany suspected, wise counsel. She desperately needed all those things at the moment, so she gathered up her skirts and hurried down the stubbled incline.

Granny's door stood wide open, reminding Bethany that Granny kept the door open so that whatever animal needed her attention could just wander in. Bethany paused in the doorway and peeked inside. Granny was, once again, at the fireplace, leaning over a large blackened pot while stirring a strange smelling concoction within the pot.

"Granny, may I come in?"

Granny turned, and upon seeing who it was, smiled gently. "Ye be welcome anytime, miss. Me an' Bella be glad ta see ye made it 'ome, what with ye hurrin' out in that terrible blo'."

Bella, the little fox Bethany had followed the day before, was still resting in her bed of straw under Granny's worktable. The little vixen chose that moment to yawn broadly. A soft whine followed, as if she were agreeing with Granny's comment.

With such a welcoming endorsement, Bethany stepped inside and immediately felt that sense of peace and safety that she had once felt at Gull Haven but was now no more.

Granny swung the big pot off the fire and turned to Bethany. Her face turned grim as she intently studied her visitor. "Somethin' be amiss. What is it, child?"

Bethany's eyes watered. "Oh, Granny, I…" She dissolved into a flood of tears.

"I be in need o' a nice cup o' tea. And by tha look o' ye, ye be needin' one too." Granny waved at the small table which was still in the center of the room. "Well, now, git along with ye and sit yerself down. Tea'll be ready afore ye know it, and then ye can start at the beginnin' an' tell Granny all about it."

The Cornish Mystique

****

Phillip, alone now in the library, sat at his grandfather's enormous desk. In front of him was the remainder of the bottle of whiskey Zeb had left there a few weeks ago. His empty glass rested a short distance away. Phillip, his jaw locked, stared at the bottle, but he didn't see it. His thoughts were elsewhere, and as black as midnight as he contemplated what had just occurred.

What had gone wrong? He had planned everything so carefully, and it wasn't as if his intentions had not been honorable. So what if he had done some maneuvering? He had not actually lied. Had he? He had just sort of left out a few minor points. But it was for the good of all. If he had married Elise, their marriage would have been miserable for both of them. And when he had become aware of the proposed displacement of Bethany…

He rose from the desk so quickly that the chair he had been sitting in nearly fell over. He simply ignored it and began a nervous pace around the room, still lost in his thoughts. She was certainly not wanted at *Belle Maison*. Indeed, she was not even wanted in England! All he was trying to do was save her from being shipped off to Ireland to a miserable existence. It wasn't as if she were the reason for her parents' death and therefore being the cause for her turning to her uncle for sanctuary. All she had done was follow her father's instructions. Just like any good daughter should at such an occasion. The lot of them should be grateful to him for solving all their problems. Instead, they acted as if he had committed some unpardonable sin.

Phillip stopped suddenly and ran a shaky hand through his hair. Hellfire, he couldn't help falling in love with the wretched girl. But that was beside the point. Surely, they did not know that. They might suspect… But it had nothing to do with the action he had taken. Surely not. Surely it was simply an attempt to right a proposed wrong.

A soft knock at the door caused Phillip to wonder if there was yet another new crisis unfolding. "Enter," he growled.

Hetty stood in the doorway, looking somewhat hesitant. "I be 'scusin' me, sir, but I thought ye might be wantin' ta know. While all that scratchin' an' clawin' was goin' on, there be one more guest what's arrived."

Phillip's head jerked up. "What? Another one?" he roared.

"It be a Mr. Adam Westcott, sir. An' 'e do say 'e be a friend o' yours."

Phillip threw himself into a nearby chair. "Dear Lord," he muttered. "Not Adam, too. Not now."

Hetty rushed forward. "Oh, it be all right, sir. I 'ave 'em all sorted out an' in their rooms, though I did 'ave ta put Mr. Westcott in with that Mr. Cavanaugh. But both gentlemen do say it be aw right." She shrugged. "But…but if'n anyone else comes along, we'll 'ave ta be nailin' 'em to tha wall."

Phillip's frustrated expression immediately softened. "Thank you, Mrs. Weddows. I hope you know how much I appreciate your efforts, with so many people arriving, and without notice."

"I learned long ago ta plan a'ead, sir. But it be Dolly, an' Lilly, an' tha new girl, Jennie, what's bein' deservin' o' yer praise. They be good workers true 'nough, an' I be right proud o' 'em."

Phillip nodded. "Of course, Mrs. Weddows, and you

are correct. Please pass on my praise, and tell them how much I appreciate their efforts."

She hesitated and shifted from one foot to the other.

"Is there something else, Mrs. Weddows?"

"Well, yes, sir, there do be somethin'. It be about supper. Aside from tha watered soup, Cook do say it'll 'ave ta be a bit o' this an' that, since we wasn't spectin' guests. She do 'ope that will be all right."

Phillip raised a sardonic brow. "If it is not, Mrs. Weddows, then my guests are welcome to go elsewhere for their meal. And they will all go with my blessing."

****

Granny, screwing up her face, made a rude noise. "An' so ye run away like a frightened little rabbit." She shook her head. "God's oath if'n I ain't ashamed o' ye."

Shocked at her response, Bethany looked up at Granny through tear-filled eyes. "But Granny, *none of it is true!* I swear. Mr. Delemere has never done anything that would cause even the most strident accuser to suspect anything unseemly might be—"

She stopped abruptly as a memory she knew she would never be able to forget crowded into her thoughts. It concerned a moonlit night, a gentle breeze slipping through a garden filled with the scent of roses, a breathtakingly handsome man standing close to her...so very close she could smell the scent of him. He had smelled of soap, cigar, and the hint of bay rum mingling with a clean, crisp fragrance. Perhaps lemon. And then there had been the delicate brush of rose petals against her cheek...

Telltale heat began to spread across her face, so she forcefully pushed the thought away. "I tell you, Mr. Delemere has always behaved in a most gentlemanly manner."

Granny raised a cynical brow. "Yes, I do see by that blush a-bloomin' in yer cheeks."

"It was nothing!" Bethany declared emphatically. "Really, it was only the simplest of gestures. He was merely being charming, I assure you. I am certain he never meant it otherwise."

"Oh, I fear no doubt that be so, 'e bein' charmin', I mean. They do say 'e be a 'andsome devil, an' thems that be that fair 'as tha devil in 'em as well. But, 'ow about ye, child? That simple gesture ye be not speakin' o', ye' ne'er think 'bout it, I s'pose?"

"Certainly, not! Well, maybe…"

Granny chuckled. "Ye be in love with 'im, my girl. An' charmin' bein' put aside, I s'pect he be in love with ye as well."

"Oh, no, Granny! That cannot be. I…I mean, look at me. I am poor, and I have no breeding to speak of. I'm just a lowly, ill-educated vicar's daughter—of no consequence. Well, yes, I am honest, and I do like to think of myself as being kind and honorable, but…well, he is a gentleman of quality! Believe me, he could never think of me in any way other than a charity case. Elise says so, and she should know."

"An' jes' who be this Elise ye speak o'?"

"She is my cousin."

Granny leaned back in her chair and studied Bethany. "Ummmm, yes, well, all that may be so, but I be thinkin' ye be forgettin' somethin' important. Two very important things." She leaned forward across the table and grasped one of Bethany's hands, which had been lying limp on the table. "Tell me somethin' child. 'Ave ye ever looked at yerself in a lookin' glass? I mean, *really* looked at yerself? Ye be a real beauty, child, not like all o' them society 'ens made up ta look like swans. And there be somethin' else. If 'e's able ta breathe, think, an' stand up on 'is own, then 'e 'as a heart, as well. An' I'll wager ever'thing I own every time 'e looks at ye, it be not yer social standin' 'e be thinkin' of."

Bethany's eyes welled up again. "He's going to marry Elise, Granny. My cousin. It has all been arranged. Everyone says so."

"Humph," Granny muttered. "An' jes' who be *ever'one?*"

Bethany shrugged. "Well, you know. Everyone of any importance in London. Then, there is his mother, Viscountess Delemere, and my aunt, Viscountess Brundridge. Even my cousin Elise says so, and she should know since she is to be his bride."

"And? Is that all?"

Bethany appeared confused. "Isn't that enough?"

"An' what o' the master? Mr. Delemere, it be, ye daft girl! What does 'e 've ta say on tha matter? I'd think 'e'd know who 'e was goin' ta wed, since 'e be the groom!"

Bethany looked away. "Mr. Delemere would never discuss such a personal matter with me. After all, I am no one of any import to him. I'm only another employee of his, although I've just discovered that is the case. It's no wonder he—"

Granny roughly shoved back her chair and stood. "Get up, with ye, girl." She waved over to where her washstand stood. "There be clean water in tha pitcher. Scrub yer face good an' there be a comb n' brush on the sill to straighten yer hair."

"But why, Granny? Am I in such disarray?"

"For what ye be 'bout ta do, *yes!*"

Bethany rose slowly. "And what is that?"

Exasperated, Granny placed her fists firmly on her hips. "Yer 'bout ta go back ta Gull Haven an' fight for tha man ye love. That's what!"

Chapter 13

It was mid-afternoon when Bethany arrived back at Gull Haven. As she entered the front door, she was met with complete silence. She paused, waiting for any indication as to the status of the situation. This was something she had not expected. Nothing stirred, no angry voices, nor even muffled bursts of laughter, nor conversations from servants going about their chores.

She quietly made her way down the hallway situated to the left of the main staircase until she reached the library. The door was ajar, so she peeked inside. What had earlier been the location of complete chaos, full of angry people with noisy accusations and denials, was now empty.

Returning to the base of the stairway leading to the upper floors, she was about to ascend when a sound like something metal hitting the flagstone floor echoed through the house. A small shriek followed. Bethany hurried down the hall toward the back of the house.

Reaching the kitchen, she took in the scene. A young girl, not more than fifteen, was on her knees frantically trying to scoop up what appeared to be a large amount of flour strewn across the flagstone floor. An upended metal bowl rested not too far away from the disaster, and bending over the poor girl, scolding her, was Mrs. Mosby, the cook. Mrs. Weddows stood just inside the doorway, observing the scene.

"Mrs. Weddows?"

Hetty turned. "Ahhhh, there ye be, miss! Praise be. I's that worried about ye, what with all tha commotion goin' on. It be a right row it were, and then ye up an' vanished."

"But…" Bethany spread her hands. "What happened?"

"Oh, that. What, indeed," Hetty muttered. "Tizzy—she be tha new kitchen girl, an' rightly named she be, I can tell ye—dropped Mrs. Mosby's pastry fixin's, an' now we 'ave a pretty mess."

"No," Bethany cried impatiently. "I mean concerning the quarrel! What has happened to everyone? There is no one about. Not even any maids. Where has everyone gone?"

"As ta that, I couldn't be sayin', miss. One minute they all be in there a-yellin' an' caterwaulin', an' then tha door burst open an' them all spilled out into tha hall like tha place be on fire, each goin' in a different direction. Doors was slammin' all over tha 'ouse, an' more yellin', an' then…nothin'."

"Do you know where Mr. Delemere is?"

"No, miss. Like I said, I do not know where any o' 'em be. I 'spect them screechin' females be in their rooms sniffin' bottles of smellin' salts while havin' them vapors what everyone talks about. Two young gentlemen come through 'ere a while back, askin' where tha stables be. I told 'em, and they 'urried out tha back door like tha devil 'isself was after 'em. As for tha master, if'n 'e 'as any sense, 'e be in tha next county by now, an' with no plans o' returnin'."

A door slammed from somewhere above stairs, startling Bethany. "Oh, Mrs. Weddows, I…I do not want to see anyone just now." She hurried toward the back door. "I think I will just go for another walk. I am not in the mood for any more unpleasantness, and besides, I…I need time to think…about, well…things."

Hetty followed her to the door. "Ye be goin' out on them heathen moors agin, I'll be wagerin', an' ye be knowin' I don't want ye out there alone. There's mischief goin' on out there, miss. Bad mischief."

Bethany didn't respond. She simply continued out the back door and once again headed straight for the moor, leaving Hetty standing in the doorway shouting her misgivings. She didn't know what else to do, or where else to go. She simply could not stand the thought of having to endure any more accusations.

Bethany slowed her pace as soon as she lost sight of Gull Haven. Plucking at the clumps of sea oats as she ambled along, she began the business of thinking about what she must do. She had to leave, of course. But oh, how the thought of doing so hurt her heart. Still, she realized that there was no other option. Granny had seen the truth immediately. Now it was time she admitted it to herself.

She was completely and hopelessly in love with her newly discovered employer. She shouldn't be surprised, for deep down in her subconsciousness, Mr. Delemere was always there. His face. His touch. His smile, and the shape of his mouth. His black silky hair… Whether awake or in her dreams, it didn't matter. She had been telling herself it was only a passing phase and would soon fade away. But she now recognized that was only a convenient lie.

Yes, she was completely and irrevocably in love with Mr. Delemere. And she knew, deep down, that she would never love another. But was he in love with her? Of course not!

The situation was quite impossible, and for more reasons than she wanted to admit. Even if Granny's belief in fairy tales were true, he would never really consider marrying a poor and humble vicar's daughter. And that is exactly what she was. Elise was quite right about that. Mr. Delemere was an aristocrat. He was handsome, wealthy, and his social standing was far above hers. He most certainly knew she would never be able to blend into his social sphere. Without knowing the proper manners, or having the sophistication which was inherent within the aristocracy, she undoubtedly would be a constant embarrassment to him. She would always say the wrong thing or use the wrong fork as she had done at *Belle Maison* on several occasions. No, it would not do. No matter how much in love with him she was, never mind the possibility of his being in love with her, she must leave immediately. If nothing else, she would surely ruin his life by being the cause of constant friction within his family if she stayed.

She rubbed her brow, hoping to wipe away a growing headache. But where could she go? She could, of course, always return to Tregony. But then what? She did have friends there, but they could not help her find employment. Tregony was nothing more than a few humble cottages sitting out in the middle of nowhere. The inhabitants were farmers, each family with their own plot of land that barely supported their household. There were no businesses there and certainly no opportunities for any type of servant, or even a companion or nursemaid. And that was probably all she was qualified to do. Now, in London…

London! She sank to the ground. Surely there would be no problem finding employment there. There were shops, and wealthy families who were always in need of servants. And she could sew! Actually, she was quite talented with a needle. Everyone said so. Yes, she nodded her head, she felt certain she could find a position as seamstress in some *modiste* shop. And depending on Mrs. Padmore's condition, if she were able to walk again, there would certainly be prospects for her in London as well. She would have to be left behind for now, but…

Apprehension quickly replaced her enthusiasm. But dare they go there? What little Bethany had seen of London was loathsome—and dangerous. The air was always filled with coal soot and the gutters with filth. Poverty was rife. Only the areas where the rich and titled resided were clean and well maintained.

Bethany barely became aware of the sound of hoofbeats before an enormous black stallion suddenly reared up out of the tall grasses surrounding her. She managed a terrifying scream and threw herself sideways just before the horse's front hooves crashed down where she had been sitting. Immediately following, an incredibly handsome but, at the moment, furious face loomed over her. And it was a familiar one.

"Faith and begorrah, ye witless *cailin*! Are ye—?" He froze. Then, slowly, a small smile appeared on his face. "'Tis *you*!"

Bethany stared up at her anonymous traveling companion, the exquisite but mysterious gentleman who had disappeared upon their first overland coach stop after leaving London.

"'Tis you!" she parroted.

His smile widened. "Aye. 'Tis me, right enough, an' since we 'ave established that yew are yew, and I am me, perhaps yew'd be good enough t' tell me if yew're okay. Lucifer dinna trample ye, did 'e?"

She looked down around her as if she expected to discover pools of blood and broken limbs strewn about. "No, I do not think so. At least nothing hurts except, perhaps, my pride."

Bethany expected him to offer her his hand and help her up off the ground. He surprised her by casually sitting down, cross-legged, beside her.

"I dunna s'pose yew'd be willin' ta tell me yer name. After all, we can't keep bumpin' inna each other an' not know who we're bumpin' inna. Dunna ye agree?" He took one of her hands, lifted it to his lips, and placed a gentle kiss on the back side of her palm.

"I am Padric Kilgallen, newly arrived from tha' wee glorious land o' Ireland. An' yew, my gel, are?"

It was then she recognized his voluminous black cape. "It was you!" she repeated.

He threw up his hands. "Awk! Do pay attention, lass. We a'ready established who I am, but—"

"No, no. I mean… You were the horseman who attempted to save me from being caught in that terrible storm."

He gave Bethany a very credible bow, even though he was sitting on the ground rather than standing. "Guilty 's charged, *colleen*. I say *colleen* for yew 'ave not, as yet, shared yer name."

Bethany felt her face flush. "Oh, I am sorry. My name is Bethany Brundridge."

"An' what, might I be askin', are ye doing sittin' out inna middlin' o' nowhere, 'idin' inna grass? Do ya not 'ave a 'ome?"

Bethany laughed. "Well, of course I have. Or, to be more precise, I should say I am, at present, residing at Gull Haven. It's just a short distance—"

"Oh, I be knowin' where 'tis." He raised a quizzical eyebrow. "Hmmm, 'ow very intriguin'. Yew 'ave gone outta yer way ta avoid statin' that Gull Haven be yer 'ome, only that yew're presently residin' there. That implies yer accommodation's only temporary."

Bethany flushed. "Yes, well, it is rather complicated."

"Wonderful!" he exclaimed. "Oh, 'ow I do love complications. They do make life so very interestin', dinna ye think?" He gently brushed away a stray curl that had settled on her cheek.

His action caused a sudden chill to sweep over Bethany, which she found odd because there was not the slightest hint of a breeze, much less a cool one.

"Now, why don' ye be tellin' me aboot this complication that's causin' such a sadness ta show on that bonny face o' yewrs?"

For the next several minutes, Bethany related to him everything that had happened to her since her father's death. She didn't know what possessed her to quite willingly share her past with a perfect stranger, except that she needed to talk to someone other than Granny. She felt that Granny was more than a little prejudiced, and perhaps a man's point of view, and especially a stranger's, might be more objective.

Once she began, she could not stop. Her immediate past, and all the ramifications that came with it, just poured out of her, even the terrible confrontation in the library that had caused her to seek peace out on the moor.

The only thing she could not share was her first meeting with Mr. Delemere on that moonlit night in a rose garden. That she would always keep safely locked away in her heart.

When she had finished, Padric Kilgallen sat there in deep thought, aimlessly plucking at the ground cover surrounding them. After what seemed like minutes of dead silence, Bethany wondered if he had forgotten she was there. She was about to remind him of her presence when he straightened, squared his shoulders, and pinned her with those beautiful, hypnotic black eyes.

"So, am I understandin' correctly? Yew're no a member of tha family residin' at Gull Haven, an' there be no emotional ties to tha family? Yer only an employee?"

Bethany hoped her face did not betray her. Why was he so interested in any personal ties she might have? Fear began to well up inside of her as she watched his face slowly take on a cunning expression. She began to feel a familiar chill. It was the same chill that had crept over her in the mail coach the first time she saw him.

Bethany knew instantly she had made a terrible mistake! That mistake had been in not trusting her instincts. She had been warned, on several occasions, that something was very wrong about him. And yet? She had confided in him. How could she have been so naïve?

"Then, I 'ave tha answer to yer dilemma, lass. And mine," he murmured. "Yew'll be comin' with me."

Bethany hoped he could not see how terrified she suddenly felt. Surely, he was joking! "I...I beg your pardon?"

"I said, yew'll be comin' with me. I've 'ad plans for yew ever since I first saw you in the mail coach. But I was not sure 'bout whatever connections yew might 'ave. A beau, parents, anyone who could be missin' ye. I 'ad ta be sure, ya see?"

Like the last piece of a puzzle put in place, Bethany realized he was the lone man out on the moor, watching, always watching, but never getting close enough to be recognized.

Too late, she understood that there was a good reason for her fear of him. That was what that chill was about every time she was around him. He was insane. Of course he was. He had to be. And she had been too trusting, and too inexperienced to see through his façade.

Just a few minutes earlier he had been so charming and pleasant that she had forgotten how wary she had been of him in the mail coach, even though he had done nothing to deserve such censure. It had been pure instinct on her part but just now, the cold, calculating look in his eyes, and the icy tone of his voice added a new dimension. They not only reflected insanity, but pure evil as well. This she knew, without a doubt, was his true nature.

She attempted to pacify him by smiling faintly in spite of the terror racing through her. "Sir, you truly are quite the humorist. But you should be very careful to whom you make such a declaration. There are some who might take you seriously."

Before she could react, he grabbed her wrist, squeezing it painfully, and roughly pulled her to him. "You *doubt* me?" His angry face slowly melted into an expression of sly triumph. "Well, no matter, my sweet. Tha time for playing these silly wee games is over. I've been watchin' ye…waitin'…for a chance to…" He smiled wickedly. "I know it's a bit early, but there'll ne'er be a better moment. Yew'll be comin' with me. Now!"

Bethany knew she had to get away, and it had to be now. Panic set in. "No! Please…. Let me go!" she cried, struggling against his grip.

His hold on her only tightened. "Let ye go? Dunna be absurd, my dearest gel. I made up me mind inna coach, when first I laid eyes upon ye. I decided, then, I'd 'ave ye for me own." He shrugged. "Oh, I admit I was lookin' for a suitable offering for Cernunnos. I always 'ave an eye out for that. But now…" His eyes took on a crazed, possessive expression. "The silly chit we 'ave now 'll 'ave ta do for Cernunnos. Yew'll be mine. In my bed, and at my beck an' call for whenever and whatever I want."

Bethany fought against growing hysteria, and she began to struggle again. "No! Please! Who…who is Cernunnos? And…and who is this *silly chit* you speak of?"

A vision of young Lucy Abney's murdered body flashed before her eyes. And now, little Alice Crumley was missing… "And what is this offering you speak of?" she whimpered, even though she already knew.

His mouth hardened, yet the rest of his features took on a rapturous quality. "Why, Cernunnos is the greatest of all the Druid gods. 'E's master o'er many things—of wealth, life, and…" He grinned wolfishly. "And fertility." He reached out and stroked her cheek with his free hand. "I knew yew'd be the perfect offering to him, and I be bettin' the others will think so too. Yew see, Cernunnos desires not only beautiful sacrifices, he desires virgins as well. But certainly not like that whinin', silly little chit we 'ave now. Oh, no. Cernunnos desires not only beautiful virgin sacrifices, 'e desires a woman full grown as well. I knew tha moment I looked at yew that yew were all three. Beautiful, completely untouched, and very much full grown." He nodded slowly. "A vicar's young sheltered dau'er…Ah yes, my sweet *colleen*, I've na doubt Cernunnos would be very pleased wi' ye. But alas, I canna resist my own desire for ye, an come tha Summer Solstice, Cernunnos, and the others 'll just have to be satisfied with that sniveling little brat we 'ave now."

Almost imperceptibly, but carried along in the wind, a faint call alerted Bethany. "Yahooooo. There be a body about? Yahoooo!"

Padric Kilgallen heard the call also. He became distracted for a split second, causing his grip on her wrist to loosen. Bethany seized that moment to jerk her hand free.

Somehow, she had the strength to stagger up even though her skirt seemed determined to tangle in her legs. In the confusion, Kilgallen attempted to grab her ankle but missed.

Once up, Bethany darted away from him while waving her arms wildly overhead. "Here! Over here!"

What seemed like an eternity but in actuality was only a minute or two passed before Ollie Smithers' delipidated wagon came clamoring toward her.

Ollie drew up his mules beside Bethany. "Why, bless ma bones if'n it ain't tha young miss from Gull Haven. Ol' Ollie, 'e do see tha 'orse, wi' no rider about, an' 'e—" His eyes squinted as he became aware of her agitation. "'ere now, what be tha matter with—"

Kilgallen suddenly appeared above the tall grass and began a mad dash toward his horse grazing nearby.

Grabbing his stallion's mane, Kilgallen leapt into the saddle and jabbed his heels into the horse's flanks.

Ollie sprang to his feet, wildly shaking a fist in the air. "'ay, there! Stop!" When Kilgallen refused to obey, Ollie could only watch the man's frantic departure before turning back to Bethany. "'Ere now, miss, what be goin' on 'ere? Who be that blighter, an' 'e didn't 'urt ya none, did 'e?"

Bethany gave him a strained smile. "N…no, Mr. Smithers. I am all right now that you are here. It was just, well, there was a misunderstanding, you see, and—" She reached up, took one of his weathered hands, and squeezed it gently. "I'm just so very grateful you came along." Releasing his hand, she straightened. "Mister Smithers, I…I know it will be a terrible inconvenience, but would you mind taking me into Newquay? Right away? It is very important."

Ollie pulled off his weathered hat and gave a thoughtful scratch to his head. "Well, miss, Ol' Ollie won't mind a bit, but he don't think yew wanna be goin' there jes now. Ever'thin' be closed up by now. It bein' so late an' all. O' course there do be tha 'Ound's 'Ead…It be open still. Now, if ye'll wait till mornin', Ol Ollie—"

"It can't wait, Mr. Smithers," she almost shrieked. "I must see the constable at once! It is very likely a matter of life and death!"

Ollie clutched his shabby hat against his chest. "Oh…but Constable Barlow, 'e not be there, miss. 'E do go with Ol' Michael Duggan, out on 'is boat for a bit o' fishin'. Ol' Charlie, that be Constable Barlow, do say 'e needs a rest from all that 'as been happenin'. Well, ye know…what with Miss Lucy, an' all. 'E did leave Jemmy Dushay ta take messages. But miss, Jemmy ain't up ta no more 'an jes' takin' messages."

Bethany froze, clutching the side of the wagon. She felt like crying. Even though Padric Kilgallen had never said so, she knew now, without a doubt, he had murdered Lucy Abney, and she also knew he had little Alice Crumley…somewhere. She was also certain that Alice was still alive because of what he had said. But for how long?

It all fit now. Padric Kilgallen had taken Alice for a sacrifice to that terrible god he had mentioned. And that is what had happened to Lucy Abney. Bethany recalled Kilgallen mentioning the Summer Solstice. When was that? June. Yes, it was sometime in June. And it was June now!

Bethany, wishing she could put a curse on Constable Barlow for leaving right in the middle of a terrible murder, rushed around to the other side of the wagon and began to climb up beside Ollie. "Please, Mr. Smithers, take me home. And hurry. Please! I've…I've got to get back home."

****

The ride back to Gull Haven had been unnaturally silent. Mr. Smithers seemed to know she needed time to think through some problem. It had been a blessing, for it had given her time to regain rational thought.

Earlier, upon learning that Constable Barlow was away, her first inclination had been to rush to Mr. Delemere and tell him of her suspicions. He would know what to do. But then, her sanity returned during their trip, and she quickly realized that was the last thing she should do. Knowing his responses to earlier emergencies, she knew Mr. Delemere would, on his own, immediately take action to save Alice from the same fate that Lucy had suffered. Bethany could not allow that to happen. That would surely put him in grave danger. She recalled Kilgallen had implied that there were others, followers, who also believed in human sacrifice. How many, she could not guess, but against only one man, there would be too many! Neither could she alert any of Newquay's menfolk. They were peaceful fishermen, for the most part. Not skilled fighters. There would certainly be bloodshed if they, disorganized, and untrained as they were, should attempt any sort of rescue. It was a certainty that Alice was well guarded.

Bethany's only option, she decided, was to tell Granny. She would know what to do, surely. Bethany immediately felt a sense of relief when she made her decision. She could do nothing now, but at first light, she would make her way to Granny's. Hopefully Granny would be home, and together they would make plans for finding and rescuing little Alice Crumley.

****

Bethany, as usual, entered Gull Haven through the back door. The kitchen, at this time of day, was alive with activity. Servants were chattering among themselves as they bustled about, breaking eggs, stirring, kneading, and chopping, all in preparation for the evening meal. Mrs. Mosby, also known as Cook, stood at the stove, checking on something bubbling in a bright copper pot. Catching a glimpse of Bethany standing in the doorway, she hurried over to her.

"Yes, miss? Ye be needin' somethin'?"

"Yes, Mrs. Mosby, if you would be so kind. I do not feel like seeing anyone just now, so I am going to my room. I am afraid I missed both breakfast and mid-meal, so I am starved. I know you are quite busy, but if you do not mind, could you please have a tray brought up to my room? I need nothing special, just some tea, maybe a bit of fruit, and perhaps some cheese."

Mrs. Mosby patted Bethany's hands, clutched against her stomach. "Certainly, miss. Now, don't ye be frettin' a bit. I be sendin' a tray up in no time."

"There is one more thing, Mrs. Mosby. I do not know where Mrs. Weddows is, so could you please tell her that I do not wish to see anyone for the rest of the day. Not even Mr. Delemere…well, especially Mr. Delemere. I plan on remaining in my room and do not wish to be disturbed."

Mrs. Mosby nodded briskly. "Aye, I understand, miss, an' I don't blame ye a bit. If'n I 'ad ma way, I'd be sendin' all them bawlin' an' whinnin' lay-abouts a-packin' back to where they come from."

Before Bethany could reply, Mrs. Mosby turned back to the kitchen and cried, "Tizzy, set a pot o' water on for tea and best ye check on them pies in tha oven. Never 'eard o' anyone likin' burnt pies."

****

Hours later, Bethany checked her bedside clock for the fourth time within an hour. She frowned, for it was not yet 10:00 p.m., and too early for bed. She was beginning to wonder if time itself had stopped. Still, she realized she should be grateful. At least the evening, so far, had gone by as she had hoped—except for one small interruption.

True to Mrs. Mosby's word, a tray had been brought up to Bethany's room, with enough food to satisfy a grown man for several days. Apparently, Mrs. Mosby had anticipated Bethany not coming down for supper, so she had made adjustments. Bethany ate her fill, then, hoping to take her mind off what might be happening to little Alice Crumley and the further danger she was in, Bethany turned to a novel, *Agnes Grey*, that she had brought all the way from Tregony. She had forgotten about having it until she found it lodged at the bottom of her valise when she unpacked at Gull Haven. Its author was one of the Brontë sisters, Ann, who had passed away before realizing how popular her effort would become. Bethany hoped a good story might take precedence over her troubling thoughts.

She had just begun the novel when there was a soft knock on her door, followed by Mr. Delemere's voice. "Miss Brundridge, please open the door. I must talk to you. I...I need to explain..." A small pause, then, "Miss Brundridge? Please. Open the door."

Bethany remained frozen in her chair until, a few moments later, she heard his footsteps fade away. After that, she tried to concentrate on Miss Brontë's novel, but to no avail. Alice's fate, as well as Mrs. Padmore's, once again mingled with the worry of where she was to go, as did the pain of leaving her newfound friends—Hetty, Zeb, Dolly, Lilly, and all the others.

She paced the floor for what seemed an eternity. When her legs began to ache from the effort, she placed a chair in front of an open window that faced the sea.

It was a lovely warm evening, moonlit, and with an unusually soft breeze blowing in from the sea. She thought perhaps watching the ever-restless waves slowly and smoothly swell into silver-crested whitecaps might ease her mind somewhat. It did not. Neither did her pacing back and forth in her darkened room. Indeed, both seemed to heighten, rather than cure, her anxiety.

What was she to do?

She knew she had no choice. She must leave Gull Haven, and before any further unpleasantness, suspicion, or accusations arose. But how? London seemed her only option. But then several new obstacles appeared in her feverish thoughts. What was she to do about Mrs. Padmore? Mrs. Padmore was still abed with her horribly injured back and the doctor was not optimistic about a quick recovery. Bethany would have to leave her companion behind, at least for a while. Then a new problem loomed. How was she to get to London? She had only a few shillings tucked away for emergencies, but not nearly enough for coach fare. She would have to walk! But London was many, many miles away. It was possible that a passing farmer or traveler might offer her a ride in their wagon, but she could not count on that. And even if she were able to get to London, what then? Lodgings were not inexpensive. Where was she to stay? How was she to seek employment, and how was she to survive until she earned her first wage?

She had foolishly assumed, earlier, that finding employment in London would be easy. Now, she realized her fallacy. It was true enough that she could certainly lose herself there. At least bodily. But her reputation would most definitely follow her. The Ladies Eugenia and Isabelle would certainly make sure all the mistresses in homes looking for servants would be aware of the tawdry little vicar's daughter and her seductive tendencies. Whether real or assumed was beside the point. No mistress would want such a temptation within such easy reach of their husbands or sons. And as for the opportunities for servants, it surely favored the employer rather than employee, even without the cloud of indiscretion hanging over a poor servant girl. There were always more applicants than jobs. And probably in London most of all.

The far-off rumble of thunder broke into her concentration, and she became aware of the sudden gusts of wind blowing in though her window. Sure enough, with the help of the nearly full moon still high in the night sky, she was able to discern dark clouds forming out over the sea, indicating yet another early summer storm was building. She hoped so, for she loved snuggling down in her bed during a storm. Most people, especially women, found storms frightening. But for her, there was something almost intoxicating about the sound of thunder, the flash of lightning, and then the constant patter of rain beating against windowpanes.

The soothing promise of rain slowly replaced her depressing thoughts as she rose from her chair and began to prepare for bed.

Chapter 14

Something startled Bethany awake. She sat up and, after several aborted attempts, finally managed to light her bedside lamp. As her bedchamber slowly became illuminated, she noticed the tintype picture of her parents, normally resting on the small table positioned at the window, was now on the floor. When a blast of wind suddenly filled the room, she realized she had left her window open and the drapes, billowing out, had brushed the picture off the table. She quickly hurried out of bed and headed for the window.

Her intent had been to shut the window. But then, the low rumble of thunder off in the distance caused her to hesitate, and she glanced outside. The storm brewing earlier in the evening was still offshore. She was thankful the inevitable rain had not yet reached land, otherwise she would have had a soggy mess to clean up.

However, that did not mean the storm was not having an effect. The sea itself had become noticeably more turbulent. What had earlier been lazy, rhythmic swells with gently moving whitecaps had now become large and angry. Their number had also greatly increased as they raced toward the shore and crashed against the base of the cliff on which Gull Haven had been built. She was not able to see their exact impact, of course, but she could not miss the fascinating results. Enormous sea sprays, one after the other, exploded above the cliff.

Bethany caught her breath for, catching the moonlight within its droplets, each spray, as it spread out, took on the appearance of a delicate, diamond-studded lace fan. The sparkling display remained in midair for only a moment, then slowly sank out of sight behind the cliff face, only to be replaced by another.

She checked the time on her clock once again. It was just after two-thirty. In less than a second, she made her decision.

Gull Haven had been built literally clinging to the side of a granite cliff. On the side facing the sea, there was nothing but a sheer drop-off into the sea itself. However, on one adjacent side, there was a pleasant area of rich soil, made even more so by the droppings from the stable. That area had been turned into a budding new vegetable garden, with already hearty young shoots of various plants sprouting from the earth. Farther down from the garden, a sloping path led to the stables themselves.

On the opposite side, a lovely stone terrace had been constructed, with French doors opening out from the house's library as well as the salon. At the edge of the terrace, a large but beautifully gnarled tree had managed to survive, providing partial shade to the terrace during the day. But it was to the edge of the cliff that Bethany was headed. A sturdy stone balustrade had been built for safety from the immediate drop-off into the sea, and it was there that the sparkling fans of spray were most prominent.

She reached the bottom floor, slipped into the darkened library, and hurried across to the French doors. It wasn't until she stepped outside that she became aware that she hadn't taken the time to either fetch her robe or find her slippers. It didn't matter, she reasoned. The night was deliciously warm and so was the wind that immediately clawed at her night rail, causing it to billow out, then swirl around her ankles. Neither was she concerned about anyone catching her in such disarray. She felt, and rightly so, that surely no one would still be up at such a late hour and certainly not with the house as dark as pitch and as silent as a grave.

****

Phillip angrily paced back and forth across his bedchamber. It had become a ritual since he had made the acquaintance of one Miss Bethany Brundridge. *Well, why should this night be any different,* he thought grumpily.

He had been pacing for the last hour or so, after spending several earlier hours tossing and turning in his bed. That, too, had become a ritual, he grudgingly conceded. He desperately wanted to go to sleep, but sleep would not come! All he wanted was a few hours of respite, but like so many other silly wishes of late, that particular one was not to be granted to him either. Why wouldn't the silly chit at least give him a chance to explain? Was she so bereft of common decency that she would not, at the very least, give him the chance to defend himself? To at least allow him to declare what his motives were?

He had just spent the most miserable, the most horrendous, evening of his life. Dinner had been a complete disaster. After several snide remarks were made by his mother and Lady Isabelle, asking where his little minion was, a deadly silence had descended around the table. The only exception had been for an occasional awkward cough followed by a loud clearing of the throat emitting from either Adam or Peter. His only relief had been after dinner, during that short duration when the men were allowed the blessed privacy to enjoy their port and cigars. However, when it was time to rejoin the ladies who had gathered in the salon, the awkwardness immediately resumed.

To her credit, Cordelia had done her best to break the pall by attempting to strike up a conversation regarding the new fashion trends which were beginning to make their appearance at Almack's. Neither of the viscountesses showed the slightest interest on the subject, nor did Elise. And certainly, the men did not. After that, Cordelia insisted they should, at the very least, test their talents at a rousing game of whist. After only a couple of hands, what little enthusiasm Elise, Adam, Cordelia, and Peter had enjoyed at the beginning of the game had completely disappeared. With that, there was little else for them to do except attempt an interest in each other.

Phillip had picked up a book only to stare at words he did not even attempt to read. The only sound in the room came from the constant click-clacking of his mother's knitting needles, flying in, out, and around a nauseating shade of yarn as if her ladyship's life depended on it, while Lady Isabelle savagely jabbed a needle in and out of a needlepoint sampler. Both broke rhythm only long enough to throw occasional visual daggers at their host.

Adam and Peter, at one point during their cigars and port, had allowed, and even encouraged, Phillip to slip from the room in order for him to go check on "his minion." Of course, that had been a useless errand because the stubborn young lady in question had refused even to answer his knock.

Still pacing his room, Phillip cringed at the memory of that effort. *Well, if that is the way she wants it…Fine!* He was through trying to help her, and he did not care if she ended up in the gutter. She was, after all, nothing to him…

He happened to look out the window without any real interest concerning the storm's approach. Something moved, catching his attention, and he came to a sudden halt. A flash of white, being whipped about by the wind, floated across the terrace below and stopped at the balustrade built at the edge of the cliff.

He had almost missed her! But there, standing in the moonlight against a backdrop of sparkling sea spray was his "minion," the little guttersnipe who meant nothing to him.

Phillip almost stumbled over a chair getting to his bedroom door.

****

Bethany felt the sea spray's soft mist as it settled on her heated cheeks and forehead. She smelled the distinct fragrance of the sea, heard the growing anger in the thunder off in the distance, and felt the tug of the wind clawing at her night rail and tossing her hair about. Suddenly the thought of leaving Cornwall, and above all leaving Gull Haven and everything she had come to love there, was too much for her. She began to cry.

This was her Cornwall! And Gull Haven was the place where she belonged. How could she leave it? And yet, she knew she must. At Gull Haven, she had found some measure of peace with a new family. Of course, no one would ever be able to take the place of her sweet mother and gently doting father. But almost immediately

Zeb and Hetty had taken her under their wing—as if she were truly their own daughter. There were Lilly, Dolly, and all the rest of the servants who had become like brothers and sisters to her in such a short time. And not to be forgotten, of course, was her amiable chaperone, Mrs. Padmore, whom she must leave behind. Bethany hadn't considered before, but what *would* become of that dear soul when she, Bethany, left? Mr. Delemere certainly would be under no obligation to keep providing bed and board for an ailing servant. She would only be a liability to him. And it was almost a certainty that Lady Isabelle would not allow Mrs. Padmore to return to *Belle Maison*. As far as Bethany had been able to learn, Mrs. Padmore had nowhere to go. She was ailing and completely alone in the world.

Yet with all the arguments Bethany could think of for staying, she knew the better of it. What became of her, and even of Mrs. Padmore, was unimportant. Mr. Delemere's reputation, his social standing within the aristocracy, and his ties with his family had to take priority over anything else. All of that would be damaged beyond repair if she remained. The poisonous gossip Elise and her mother would spew, without doubt, among their peers would surely earn Mr. Delemere *persona non grata* in any and all good society. No, she must not allow that to happen. She would not!

"Bethany."

It was nothing more than a whisper in the wind. Soft and pleading. At first, she assumed it was her imagination because she was, as always, thinking of him. He was always there, in the deepest, most secret recesses of her being.

But then she heard her name again.

"Bethany, please. Turn around and look at me. You must give me a chance to explain."

Her heart began to pound recklessly, for she now realized it was not her imagination. She slowly did as he asked.

If her heart had been pounding before, when she caught sight of him, it began to slam against her ribs. He stood only a few paces away, bathed in moonlight, and he was half naked!

She had never before seen a man without his being fully clothed. Now, she could not take her eyes away from the one before her. He stood there bare-chested and barefooted. The only thing between was what she recognized from her father's laundry as a pair of gentleman's unmentionables.

They remained facing each other, rooted to the ground, for either a few seconds or an eternity, Bethany was not sure.

Finally, he muttered, "Aww, Judas be damned," and he rushed toward her.

Bethany found herself enveloped in his arms, crushed against his torso, his dark chest hair tickling her cheek.

Resistance never occurred to her. She willingly succumbed to the delicious feel and strength of his warm, muscled flesh while from somewhere within her intoxicated brain she became aware of his lips placing slow, languid kisses in the crook of her neck. His mouth moved lazily up to her ear, then trailed across her jaw until… She only managed a small, surrendering sigh, before his mouth completely silenced her.

Of their own volition, Bethany's arms slipped around his neck and, although she had never been kissed before, she returned his caresses with every bit as much passion as he was giving. She could not help it. It was like a dam bursting. She did not care whether her behavior was unladylike or not. This was the culmination of all her dreams since that one lovely night in a moonlit rose garden when he had ever so delicately brushed her cheek with the petals of a rose.

Too soon, his lips left hers. "Bethany, please understand," he murmured. "I never meant to put you into any sort of compromising position. I was only trying to help you. That night, in your uncle's rose garden, I had just come from a very enlightening encounter with Elise. In her arrogance, she more than adequately made clear her feelings toward you. And then, as if that weren't enough, she proceeded to tell me of the plan she and Isabella had for shipping you off to Ireland. Bethany, I knew you would hate that. And... oh, I will not go into detail, but shortly afterward I discovered I had a library that needed organizing. I knew you loved books, or at least you liked to read, because on several occasions I noticed you holding one or more books. And oh, I don't know, it just seemed that, all of a sudden, the solution to everyone's problem fell into place. The fact that you were missing Cornwall so much, and my library, being in Cornwall, needing to be put in order... Well, it just seemed the perfect solution."

Pulling back, she studied him through tear-filled eyes. "I know you meant no harm, Mr. Delemere. You were merely being kind. But why did you not just tell the truth? Why go through such an elaborate ruse? Why blatantly lie to so many people?"

Phillip looked taken aback. "Lie? Lie? Tell me one thing that I lied about." When she didn't answer immediately, he continued, "Can you truthfully say that any one of them, your aunt or uncle, Elise, my family, and yes, even *you*, would have readily agreed to such an offer?"

Again, she remained silent.

He nodded angrily and growled, "Uhhhh. *Now* you are beginning to understand. I did not lie about anything. I just gave them the essentials and left out the details. What is wrong with that? I gave them the information they needed to make an *unbiased* decision. If I had muddied the waters, so to speak, and elaborated as to who your prospective employer was to be, their prejudices, and no doubt their runaway imaginations, would have completely influenced their judgment—and not for the better. I can assure you, if I had done anything differently, we would not be standing here. By now, you would be well on your way to Ireland, and I would still be in need of someone to reorganize my library."

Somehow, she had the presence of mind to pull out of his arms. She knew he spoke the truth, but she was still firm in her resolve. She must never play a part in a scandal that would surely damage his reputation in a world she could never be a part of. Oh, certainly, the young blades and the old rakes of the *ton,* with smirks on their faces, would wink and pat him on the back during a night of cards in their wretched clubs. But no respectable matron or anxious mother searching for a suitable husband for her daughter would ever consider receiving him.

"It does not matter," she replied wearily. "None of it matters now, because, regardless of what was said and what was intended, the fact remains…I must leave. And I must do so immediately."

Bethany had managed to take a few steps backward, until her back collided with the balustrade. Phillip took advantage of the moment and, matching her steps, he quickly gathered her up in his arms once again.

"You will do no such thing," he murmured into her hair. "Jesus, Bethany, have you not realized it yet? Have you not noticed how helplessly and hopelessly in love with you I am? Ever since that night in Hamilton's rose garden I have not been able to think or sleep or even reason without you being in my thoughts. I am so besotted that sometimes I think you are the only reason I am still breathing. But if you ever leave me, I know, without a doubt, I will end up a lonely and embittered old man, for I shall never love another."

It was then both Bethany and Phillip became aware of a thoroughly malicious chuckle. From somewhere within the deep shadows mottling the terrace came a very poisonous but nevertheless recognizable voice.

"Well, well, what do we have here? The two of you, here, alone in the moonlight, and both of you, well...*déshabillé!*"

Chapter 15

The sun had not quite cleared the horizon when Bethany slipped out the front door. Normally, she would have left by the back door. That had always been her normal entrance and exit from Gull Haven. But this morning she had heard Mrs. Mosby already bustling about in the kitchen.

She quietly closed the front door, turned, and looked around. She wanted to make sure no one observed her departure.

It promised to be a lovely day. The latest summer storm had been of short duration, and not as violent as those previously. Now, just before dawn, there was not a cloud in the sky. However, that did not mean everything was not rain-drenched. She carefully avoided the random puddles dotting the gravel drive, then stepped out onto the lush wet lawn. Granny's cottage was only a scant three miles away, and Bethany would be there well before she was missed at Gull Haven.

She had just cleared the first rise away from Gull Haven when the sun's rays burst onto the landscape. She stopped and took in a deep breath. Everything looked so bright and fresh. She only wished she felt the same way.

Her energy had sagged significantly, as she had not had any sleep since earlier that night. Even then it had been restless and interrupted long before the fall of her parents' picture to the floor had awakened her.

Immediately following came the unexpected encounter with Mr. Delemere, when all her wildest dreams had come true. He had taken her into his arms, held her gently, sweetly, and yet so hungrily that she thought her heart would surely burst from happiness. And there was more! He had kissed her and confessed the depth of his love for her. It had been more than she could ever have dreamed possible, until...

Elise! Her sudden appearance and the horrible things she had said! What her cousin had called her was unimportant. But what Elise had threatened to do to Mr. Delemere's reputation was beyond hateful. She had promised to spread vile accusations concerning his behavior with the vulgar little wanton he had deliberately taken into his home. A home that was in actuality nothing more than a house of debauchery, or so Elise stated.

The heavy valise Bethany held in her hand, containing everything she possessed, suddenly became too heavy to bear. She allowed it to fall to the ground. Bending over, she clutched her knees, and took in another deep breath. Oh, how she wished she could just lie down and sleep for a few more hours. Just enough to renew her energy. But she knew that was impossible. So much depended on her staying on her feet. Alice's life hung in the balance. So was Mr. Delemere's reputation, and she had to keep going for her own good as well. She needed to disappear, start over, and begin a new life. After hopefully rescuing Alice from Padric Kilgallen, it was imperative that she reach London as soon as may be. She had to find some sort of employment, for all she had in her pocket were a few shillings for food and lodging. That would not last long, and by the time she reached

London, it would have been spent and she would have nothing at all.

With new resolve, she picked up her valise and continued on. If she could just get to Granny's, she was certain Granny would allow her to take a short nap—in fact, she would insist upon it. Afterward, they would make plans to somehow locate Alice and rescue her.

What seemed like ages later, the last of her energy spent, Bethany could not take another step. Her eyelids felt made of lead. She noticed a small rock outcrop just a few yards away and, with her last bit of determination, she hurried over to it. Dropping her valise once again, she sank to the ground. Just a few minutes' sleep…that was all she needed.

Sometime later, she was aroused from a deep sleep by something, or someone, lifting her head up. But before she could come to her senses, a cloth was pressed over her nose and mouth. There was a strange odor, she felt as if she could not get her breath, and then…she fell into darkness.

****

Phillip dropped his plate onto the dining room table, threw himself into the accompanying chair, and slumped over his breakfast. He felt as if he'd been dragged behind a horse for several miles. And why not, he thought gloomily. After that horrendous scene on the terrace just a few hours earlier, with little to no sleep afterward, it was a small wonder he did not feel worse. He picked up his fork and began to pick at the eggs on his plate, but without any real interest in them.

Lord! It had been horrendous. He would never have believed Elise capable of spewing such venom. Yet he had witnessed it first hand. And that had not been all. If

Adam, hovering in the background, had not been with her to physically restrain her, Phillip was certain she would have attacked both himself and Bethany. And with those always well-groomed long nails of hers, he was certain she would have inflicted some profoundly serious wounds on both of them.

And that was something else! Just what were Adam and Elise doing alone, together, in the middle of the night? It seemed to him as if she had some explaining to do herself before she had a right to spread aspersions concerning anyone else.

But it was Bethany he was most concerned about. Even in the moonlight Phillip had been able to see her face reflecting first sheer horror, then embarrassment, and finally utter humiliation, none of which she deserved, before she ran headlong back into the house.

"Excusin' me, sir, but ye not be eatin'. Be there somethin' amiss wi' yer food?"

Phillip slowly looked up and found Tizzy, one of the kitchen maids, standing beside him. She looked nervous, for her hands were clutched together tightly, and she was avoiding eye contact with him.

"Can I be gettin' ye somethin' else, sir?"

Phillip studied her closely. Something was definitely amiss. It was unheard of for a kitchen maid to appear outside of the kitchen, and certainly not serving at table. Normally it was a footman who oversaw meals. Then it hit him. Of course! Last evening's debacle was probably being discussed and speculated about between the servants, causing their normal routine and chores to be disrupted.

Phillip, pushing back his chair, tossed his napkin to the table. He had had enough. He was weary of

The Cornish Mystique

deception, of quarreling relatives, dancing around issues, and now chaos among his servants' duties. Bethany was going to listen to his side of the story. Again. And she was going to hear it over and over until she truly understood his motives. And she was going to do so without any more delays. "No, uh...Tizzy, is it? You may not get me anything else, but you can certainly have Dolly deliver a message for me. Please tell her to tell Miss Brundridge that I wish...no! Tell her to say I demand to see Miss Brundridge as soon as may be, and that I will bridge no argument for her not complying. Dolly is to tell Miss Brundridge that she will listen to what I have to say, and she will do so without any more delays. Is that understood?"

Tizzy swallowed with difficulty and dipped him a slight curtsy. "Y-yes, sir, it be understood. But, well, which Miss Brundridge do Dolly be tellin'? There be more 'an one now."

"Miss Bethany Brundridge, Tizzy," he snapped, giving her a vague wave of dismissal. "And be quick about it."

Tizzy did not move.

Phillip darted a fierce scowl in her direction. "Well? What are you waiting for? I said be quick about it."

Tizzy clutched her nervous hands. "Well, sir, I be tellin' Dolly aw right, but she can't be doin' what yew want."

"And may I ask why not?"

Tears began to fill Tizzy's eyes. "Well, b'cause, ya see...Mi-Miss Bethany be gone, sir."

Phillip was furious. "And just where, may I ask, has she gone at this time of day?"

"I'll not be knowin', sir. Me an' Dolly, we jes be

servants. It not be our place ta…"

Now Phillip knew something was terribly wrong. A horrible feeling began to settle over him, and he muttered threateningly, "Just what is it you are not telling me, Tizzy?"

Like a dam bursting, Tizzy cried, "Oh, sir, she be gone! Miss Bethany, she be really gone. All 'er clothes, the picture o' 'er Mam and Da…even 'er Bible. Dolly do say that ever'thin's gone."

Before Tizzy could catch her breath, Phillip exploded from his chair and rushed from the room, yelling, "Mrs. Weddows!"

Tizzy quickly followed in his wake and nearly ran into him when he stopped suddenly at the library. He turned to her.

"Tizzy, go find Mrs. Weddows. Tell her I want every employee at Gull Haven, inside and out, to gather in the library. Posthaste!" He waved a hand wildly. "I do not care what they are doing. They are to stop immediately and obey my summons. In the kitchen, if they have something on the stove, they are to take it off the fire or let it burn. I do not care which."

Phillip happened to catch sight of his mother, Lady Isabelle, and Elise, standing together on the stairs leading up to the second floor. Each had their noses high in the air, and all with superior expressions on their faces.

"And you!" He shook a furious finger at them. "I have a few words for the three of you. All three of you are to return to your rooms. Repack your cases. And you'd better be quick about it because I want all three of you presumptuous and hate-filled busybodies out of my house within the hour. Is that perfectly clear? And what is more, from now on the three of you may consider yourselves no longer welcome at Gull Haven until you are otherwise notified by me. Is that also clear?"

His mother began to descend the stairs. "My dear Phillip, do behave yourself. What is all this absurd shouting about? Your little tempers are becoming quite tiresome, to be sure."

"Stop right there, Mother. Perhaps you did not hear me clearly. I have told you to go pack your belongings and be on your way back to London. You are no longer welcome here."

Lady Delemere glared at her son. "Stop this nonsense, Phillip. At once! I am your mother, and I—"

"And this is *my* home. Not yours. Please try to remember that."

Her ladyship merely shrugged. "Well, of course, what you propose is quite impossible, in any case. I strongly suspect that Cordelia has not even awakened yet. And neither have Mr. Cavanaugh nor Mr. Westcott. Why, we have not even had our morning tea yet!"

Phillip, crossing his arms across his chest, glared at his mother. "Mama, you may have your morning tea, and as much of it as you can swallow, wherever you please—as long as it is not here. And as for that hoyden little sister of mine, she is more than welcome to stay—for as long as she pleases. She may also sleep the day away as far as I am concerned. That also applies to Peter and Adam. They may also stay for as long as they wish." His face suddenly soured. "As a matter of fact, I strongly suspect that I shall be needing all of them in the coming days."

And with that, he turned on his heel and headed down the hall.

An hour later, the library was crowded with Phillip's employees at Gull Haven. From gardeners to stable boys, to kitchen maids, they all naturally huddled together in groups according to their respective positions. And from each group a low but steady hum filled the air as they murmured among themselves as to the reason for this most unusual summons.

Phillip threaded his way through the crowd, and upon reaching his grandfather's large desk, he picked up a heavy paperweight and banged it several times against the desktop. "Ladies and gentlemen, may I have quiet, please?"

Slowly, the crowd became hushed.

Phillip began to pace back and forth in front of the desk. "Some of you, I am sure, if you have not already been told, are wondering why you have been summoned here *en masse* without any prior notice." A low rumble rose throughout the room, and heads began to nod. Phillip waved a silencing hand to quiet them. "Rest assured it is not because any of you are about to be relieved of your duties. It is because I need information, and I will be needing your help, as well."

He paused from speaking but continued his aimless pacing. "For those of you who may not be aware, Miss Bethany Brundridge has left Gull Haven. It is assumed she left sometime during the night, and she left without giving anyone notice and without leaving any hint as to where she intended to go."

Again, a low hum rose within the crowd. Then, one of the gardeners raised his hand.

"Be excusin' me, sir, but…what did tha miss do?"

Phillip immediately realized his employees must be assuming she had committed some crime. Probably theft, since that was the most common offense among servants. He shook his head furiously. "No. No. It is not what all of you are assuming. Miss Brundridge did nothing wrong, Mister, Mister, uh…"

Someone called out, "'e be Lewty Burrows, sir."

"She did nothing wrong, Mr. Burrows. She was driven away because of unfounded and inaccurate accusations, all of which she is completely innocent of committing."

The murmurs began once more, and again Phillip raised his hand to silence them. "Listen to me, please. Given the circumstances of late, by that I mean the unexpected disappearance and tragic death of Miss Abney, and now the disappearance of Miss Crumley, one cannot ignore the real possibility that the same fate might very well befall Miss Brundridge. I believe with an almost certainty that Miss Brundridge had no money of any consequence in her possession, and I know for a fact that she has no relations to turn to. She is alone in this world. She will surely suffer an unpleasant fate under those conditions, unless she is found."

Heads began to nod, and the murmurs returned.

Phillip raised his voice. "I am going to need your help in finding her."

Immediately the crowd stilled and became quiet.

"Right now, I need information. First of all, did anyone happen to see Miss Brundridge leave? And if you did, did you notice what direction she took? Did she meet up with anyone?"

Almost to the last man and woman, everyone shook their head implying no.

"Do you know if she made any friends in the vicinity? Anyone she might go to for help, or possibly to seek refuge?" Even as he said the words, the image of the black-caped man who had abandoned her out on the moor crowded into his already harried thoughts. He had never been able to forget the man and had never stopped wondering what his connection was to Bethany. She had claimed she did not know the man. But had she been telling the truth?

From somewhere within the crowd a voice called out, "Well, sir, there do be Granny Faunus."

Phillip's head snapped around. "Who said that?"

From the back of the room, a familiar face threaded its way through the crowd until a tall but stooped old man stood face to face with Phillip.

"It be me, sir, Ol' Ollie Smithers. I be in tha kitchen, 'avin' myself a cup o' coffee, when someone do say ta come in 'ere right away. So 'ere I be. Ya see I 'ad jus' delivered a batch o' fixin's ta—"

"Never mind that, Mr. Smithers," Phillip interrupted irritably. "Just tell me about this Granny Faunus. Who is she, and where does she live? Does she live near here? Is it possible Miss Brundridge might have gone there?"

Ollie, shaking his head, waved his hands in a negative gesture. "No, no, sir. It not be 'bout tha missin' miss maybe bein' at Granny's. Ya see, Granny be gone. She be near Pirate's Cove, seein' to a sick friend jus' now. No, it be somethin' else that I be thinkin' yew ought ta know. It be 'bout a strange bird, a man, wearin' a big black cape, an' ridin' a stallion black as sin."

Phillip felt as if he could not get his breath. He knew it! He knew there was something not right about the man who had left Bethany lying unconscious out on the moors with a vicious storm approaching.

He grabbed Ollie's arm and squeezed. "Mr. Smithers, what do you know about this man? You must tell me everything. Do not leave anything out."

Ollie, with his free hand, scratched his head thoughtfully. "Well now, let me think on it. We first took notice o' 'im—"

Phillip shook Ollie's arm. "Who, Mr. Smithers? Who is, 'we'?"

Ollie shrugged. Well, you know, me an' most o' tha town folk in Newquay. Some weeks back, it be. He come ridin' inta Newquay on that big black beast o' his, an' with a big wagon followin'. That day 'e do spend a good amount o' time, goin' ta first one business, then t'other. Buyin' all manner of goods, 'e was."

"What kind of goods, Mr. Smithers?"

Ollie shrugged again. "Ever'thin'. Lumber, nails, shovels, picks... Then, 'e nearly bought up all the dry goods in ol' Charlie Wiggins' store."

"What did he buy there?"

"Bessie, that be Charlie's missus, do say 'e bought ever'thin' from dishes ta blankets. Same with food parcels. Ol' Jacob Townsend do say he bought up a good amount o' food stuffs—enough, Jacob do say, ta feed a dozen people for a week or more. An' since then, 'e comes in like cat ta cream, an' buys more."

Phillip suddenly remembered a conversation he'd had with his father. Something about a maniac in Ireland who was going around kidnapping young women, then killing them in some grotesque way. His father, reading from the paper, stated that the authorities believed he, and a group of his followers, had fled the country, because the killings had suddenly stopped. Unfortunately, those same authorities had no idea where they had fled.

Phillip's heart began to pound. Well, he certainly did. He had a very good idea where they had fled. It was to England, and they had settled in Cornwall where they had resumed their sadistic rituals on fresh ground. It had to be! And their leader? He always wore an elaborate black cape and rode a large black stallion. Of course it was. First there was Lucy Abney, found floating in the harbor with her heart cut out. Then little Alice Crumley went missing. Was she still alive? He doubted it. And now…? He had almost had Bethany on the day of that terrible storm. If she had not fallen off his horse, and Phillip had not come upon them… That was why the mystery man had fled, leaving her unconscious on the ground. He did not want to be known!

Phillip grabbed Ollie by the shoulders and shook him firmly. "Mr. Smithers, now think carefully. Do you have any idea where this black-caped man might have set up housekeeping?"

Ollie thought for a moment. "Well, no, sir. Ol' Ollie don't know for certain, but 'e do think it be somewhere north o' 'ere."

"Why do you think so?"

"Well sir, it be 'cause that do be tha direction 'e do come an' go. An Ol' Ollie always do see 'im ridin' like the devil wuz after 'im going back an' forth along the cliff path, an' with a big black cape aflappin' in tha breeze behind 'im."

Chapter 16

Bethany, although extremely drowsy, became aware of her surroundings. She found herself in a large bed, in a very dark room with a single candle burning on a wooden crate beside the bed…and she was completely naked! She attempted to sit up, but floundered, her body failing to obey.

From somewhere within the darkly shadowed room came, "Ahhh, so ya be awake at last." There was a rustling sound, then an extremely tall but very thin woman appeared above her. The woman's face was wrinkled, like that of an old woman, but her eyes, almost lost in their sockets, were black as night, yet seemed to glow with a feverish intensity belying old age.

"'ow ye feel, *colleen*?" She placed an almost skeletal hand, complete with jagged, unkept nails, on Bethany's forehead. "Ahhh, that be good. No fever."

"Where…where am I?" Bethany managed to ask, "And who are you? And…and where are my clothes!"

The woman cackled softly. "Aye, ye may well ask, *colleen*. My name is Morina, an' tha clothes ye be wearin' were aul wet an' muddy. But no matter. Ye'll not be in need o' 'em anymore. An' as ta where ye be? Ye be in Kabos's lair." Smiling, she exposed a mouth missing several teeth. "Ai, 'nd that reminds me…" She turned and started for the door.

Bethany, still abed, jerked to a sitting position.

"Wait! Who…who is this Kabos person, an-and how did I get here? What happened to me?"

The woman stopped and turned. "Who is Kabos, you ask?" Her aged face took on an serious expression. "Why, he be tha all-knowing one. Our leader, our teacher, and the messenger from our gods. And as for the rest o' yer questions…" She began to cackle. "Oh, yu'll be findin' out soon enough, *cailin*. Yes, indeed. Yu'll be findin' out soon enough."

Bethany watched the woman, Morina, disappear through the doorway. The solid wooden door shut with a thud, followed by the sound of a heavy metal key turning in the lock.

As soon as she was sure Morina had gone, Bethany crawled from the bed as best she could. Still groggy, she managed to pull on the white monk's robe lying at the foot of the bed. Then she awkwardly grabbed the candle from the bedside table and half hurried, half stumbled toward a pair of thick black drapes.

Bethany flung open the drapes, expecting to find a window from which she might be able to discern where she was and possibly escape. She was immediately disappointed. The wide window she expected turned out to be nothing but an arrow-slit, a long, narrow break in the rock wall, probably ten feet tall, but not more than five to perhaps seven inches wide.

She was in some sort of ancient castle or long-ago-abandoned fortification, and it was by the sea. She could smell the salty sea air floating in through the slit. But she would never be able to make her escape through such a narrow space.

She recalled someone telling her that along Cornwall's coastline several ancient strongholds had been built during ancient times. They were placed to ward off any invaders that might approach from the sea. As time passed, and with the threat of invasion dwindling, the Cornish coast became a favorite place for pirates to land and stash their ill-gotten goods in these fortifications. With all their hidden cubbyholes, nooks, and crannies, they were a perfect place for the pirates to store their goods. There were also several deep caves below the cliffs, carved out by the ocean, where freebooters would stack their smuggled barrels and crates of liquor.

Even with all that information, she still did not know where she was. The Cornish coast consisted of many miles, stretching from just north of Bude on the northwest side, down and around Land's End, then northeast up to near Plymouth.

Her heart began to pound recklessly. She could be anywhere!

The salt air had almost completely cleared her head, so she hurried back to the bed, sat down, and began to form a plan of escape. She quickly realized that the only possible way of escape was to overpower the next person to step through the door. But how was she to do that? She barely weighed eight stone. If Morina returned, Bethany was not worried, but if someone else walked through the door, weighing twice as much…

The grating sound of a key slipping into the lock in the door startled Bethany. Almost without thinking, she quickly extinguished the candle, tossed it away, and grabbed the heavy candleholder. Then she headed for the door.

The door swung open, and Padric Kilgallen stepped into the room.

****

Bending over Phillip, Ollie gently shook him. "Mr. Delemere, sir, ol' Ollie do think yew best wake up now."

Phillip and Ollie were completely hidden within tall grass growing up an incline facing an ancient fortress. It was the fourth such structure they had found scattered along the western Cornish coastline. The first three had been completely uninhabitable, not much more than huge piles of rubble. Then they'd happened upon this fourth one, which possessed a still-standing substantial turret with, off to its left, a wing of what appeared to be a row of rooms with their doors still attached. There was also evidence of the compound being inhabited, for there was a small cart and a rather large pile of wood occupying what used to be an enclosed courtyard. However, by then there was nothing left of Phillip's endurance. He had told Ollie he needed to sit down for a moment to rest. That was just before sundown. He had not meant to fall asleep. Nevertheless, it had been so long since he'd had any rest, and his body had simply rebelled. When Phillip sat down and sank back within the grass, he had fallen asleep from utter exhaustion.

Hearing Ollie's voice, Phillip immediately jerked to a sitting position. "What? Yes! Is…is something happening?"

Phillip felt like he had been run over by a runaway carriage. His marathon of sleeplessness had begun just prior to his finding Bethany out on the terrace watching the sea spray. He had not been able to sleep earlier because he had been busy mentally berating her for not allowing him to explain his somewhat dubious half-truths. It certainly continued on after that horrible encounter with Elise. Then, at the breakfast table, he had discovered Bethany had bolted. He could not blame her, but then came the frantic need to find her. That caused him to order the meeting in his library, and after Ollie had revealed his best guess as to where the black-caped mystery man might have set up housekeeping, there was no help for it. Phillip simply had to formulate and organize a plan to find and rescue her.

He shook his head, then rubbed his bleary eyes. "What time is it, Mr. Smithers?"

Ollie pulled out his watch. With the moonlight, he read the time. "It be gettin' close ta midnight, sir. An' ta answer yer question…ol' Ollie 'as ta say, yes and no."

"Well, spit it out, man! Did you see her? Miss Brundridge?"

"Well…no. Ol' Ollie don't see tha miss. But 'e do see somethin'. It be a mite ago Ol Ollie be lookin' ov'r tha place, an' 'e 'appen ta see a bit o' light there." He pointed at the only intact turret amid the crumbling structure. "It be like a candle shinin' out o' tha wall, an' then, it be gone."

Phillip crouched on his knees. "Where in the wall, Mr. Smithers? Tell me."

Once again Ollie pointed to the only standing turret. "It be a mite below tha top o'… Well, bless ma bones. Look!"

Moonlight shone on a lone figure standing on the roof of the turret. The figure remained motionless for a moment, then began a slow pace along the edge of the roof, scanning the area.

"Have you seen anything else suspicious, Ollie? I mean, he could be just an innocent watchman hired by someone to guard any number of things kept inside for safekeeping. We can't just attack someone for doing his job. We need to be sure."

Ollie scratched his head. "Well, if'n that be so, then 'e come 'ere on a big black stallion what's been grazin' close by. Ya can't see 'im 'cause it be dark. But, 'e's there, all right. An' 'e 'as company. There be other 'orses with 'im, and a big wagon is sittin' around tha side. Ya can't see it from 'ere."

"Okay, Ollie," Phillip muttered. "That is good enough for me. A light coming from an abandoned turret? A big black stallion, along with other horses, and…a big wagon, you said? Tell me, Mr. Smithers, would you say it was large enough to haul all manner of house goods?"

Ollie nodded. "That be so, sir. Sure enough. An' it still be full o' all matter of boxes an' barrels an' such."

Phillip, raised up enough to glance around above the tall grass. "Blast! Where is everyone, Ollie? Is there no one else coming?"

Ollie, grinning, nodded vigorously. "Oh, yes, sir, an' there be a whole passel of 'em. Constable Barlow, he do come back from fishin' with ol' Michael Duggan, an' 'im sent out Michael and Jemmy Dushay ta gather up all tha town folk what might be willin' ta come an' 'elp. Looks like it be almost 'alf tha town that come. They not be forgetting what 'appened to little Lucy Abney, and now they know them 'eathens 'as our Alice."

"But where are they, Mr. Smithers? I do not see—"

"Oh, well, not to worry, sir. After yew drifted off ta sleep I went an' met up with 'em on the road. They left all their wagons an' 'orses back down tha road a piece. Now, they be scattered all around, 'idden 'ere in tha tall grass an' bushes an' all. We jus' be waitin' for yer signal, an we'll pile in on 'em nest o' vipers like fleas on a ugly dog."

Phillip hesitated for a moment, then muttered, "Not just yet, Mr. Smithers. Before we do anything, I need to slip in there. Alone. I need to find Miss Brundridge first and make sure she is out of harm's way. If we start a fight prematurely, they might…they might kill her before we can free her."

Ollie nodded. "Ahhh, that shor be true. Ol' Ollie ne'r thought o' that. And 'ow 'bout our little Alice Crumley? Would ya be lookin' for 'er too?"

"Her, too, Mr. Smithers. That is a promise."

****

Bethany stood paralyzed for a moment. She could not believe her good luck. Padric had not been expecting a surprise attack, and as he stepped into the room, she had managed to knock him out with one blow. And miracle of miracles, the candle he had been holding, although knocked from its holder, was lying on the floor, still lit.

She quickly retrieved the sputtering candle, stuffed it into the heavy candleholder she had knocked him out with, then set it well out of the way. Grabbing one of Padric's wrists, she dragged him well into the room before confiscating the key still in the lock. She stuffed it into one of the pockets of the robe she wore, and closed the door.

She quickly scanned the room but could not find anything resembling or ready to serve as rope, so she wasted no time. She tore strips of cloth from the bedding and used them to tie Padric's feet and hands together behind his back. She finished by gagging him, for good measure.

As soon as she was sure she had done all she could

to disable Padric, Bethany quickly and silently slipped from the room, locked the door behind her, and disappeared down a long, narrow stone stairway in search of Alice Crumley.

****

Phillip, lost in the shadows, hugged the wall of the remaining turret. He had waited until the watchman above had turned to walk away from the front of the turret. Then, he had slipped down the slope and across the worn roadway to cling to the roughened stone wall. Earlier, he had spotted what looked like a small opening near the turret's base. He wasn't sure what it was, but it appeared large enough for him to squeeze through.

It turned out to be some sort of air vent. It was barred, but because of time and rust, he was able to make short work of removing its covering.

As expected, he found himself in total darkness inside, although he had a sense of being in a large but cluttered space. He began to feel about. Luckily, he discovered an old torch lying on what felt like a large wooden crate of some kind. He dug around in his pockets until he found one of the newfangled self-igniting matches that were quickly becoming so popular, although still in short supply. Within seconds, he found himself in what was apparently a storage room.

Crates of every size were piled about, some open, some empty, and some in the process of being emptied. He raised the torch, searched, and noticed a door that hopefully was a way out. He was not disappointed.

He found himself in another room, much smaller than the one he had just left, and this one was completely empty. There were two doors on the far side of the room and a roughly chiseled stone staircase spiraling upward.

He headed for the door near the staircase.

Slowly opening the heavy, ancient door, he peeked out to see what lay beyond. The door opened onto the large courtyard they had spotted earlier, where the small cart and pile of wood were located. And that is when he became aware of a low rhythmic hum.

Deep and mournful, it took him a minute to recognize it as some sort of chant. The sound chilled him to the bone. He wanted to discover its source, so he stepped through the door just in time to see a group of white-robed individuals appear out of an opening he had not noticed. He quickly stepped back through the door and extinguished his torch.

As if hypnotized, the group moved single file in step with the rhythmic chant. Each carried an arm full of logs and wooden branches of various sizes. Phillip gave a sigh of relief that they apparently had not noticed him, but he was curious as to what they were up to. He quickly relit his torch and followed at a safe distance behind them. When the strange procession rounded a corner, Phillip held back but carefully peered around the corner.

The chanting group seemed to float over the remains of what had been yet another stone wall, then continued on until they arrived at an open area resembling but much smaller than the original courtyard. A makeshift altar had been built off to one side, with an assortment of odd-looking objects placed on its surface. He recognized the skull of either a sheep or a goat, several small statues, a shallow bowl, and other objects he could not identify from his distance.

His concentration was diverted from the altar and back to the procession when, one by one, the chanters began to dump their loads of wood into a small shallow pit positioned in the center of the area.

A bonfire? But for what purpose? And then another thought struck him. It looked very much like some sort of ritual was about to take place, and he bet everything he owned that it was not going to be a pleasant affair. *Could it be…?*

Lucy Abney had been found not long after her death. It was obvious her remains had not been meant to be found at all. They had tossed her body into the bay, most likely thinking the tide would carry her out to sea. If it had not been for that storm… Had they decided on a new, more thorough way to dispose of what was left after being sacrificed?

Phillip's blood turned to ice as he swung around and ran headlong back to the empty room. He had to find Bethany! Now! Before it was too late…

He all but skidded to a stop in the middle of the empty room. Turning, he once again stared at the two doors. One, he knew, opened onto what had been a courtyard. The other had to lead below ground, most probably to a dungeon of sorts. Then, he glanced at the stone stairway clinging to the interior wall. It spiraled upward to…where? Ollie had seen a light within the stone façade, farther up.

Phillip began to reason it all out and almost immediately dismissed the likely dungeon. Surely, they would not leave a precious sacrifice in a filthy dungeon. They would make certain she was as clean and pristine as possible if she were to be a sacrificial gift to whoever or whatever they worshiped. Therefore, logic told him she had to be somewhere above rather than below.

He raced toward the bottom of the stone stairway.

****

Bethany crept along the darkened hallway, hoping she would not run into one of her captors. She discovered there were four rooms on the floor she was on, and each one was sealed with a heavy wooden door, exactly like the one to the room where she had been imprisoned. Stopping at each door, she put her ear to each roughened surface, hoping to hear some evidence of Alice's presence inside, or any sound of movement. Met with complete silence at each door, she continued on down the stairs.

Two floors down, she was repeating the process when, at the third door, she thought she heard something…a soft sob, followed by the distinct sound of weeping.

"Alice?" Bethany uttered softly into the crack between the roughened door and the doorframe.

The weeping suddenly stopped, followed by complete silence. "Alice, you do not know me. We have never met, but I am a friend."

Bethany recognized some sort of shuffling. Then, right up against the door, she heard, "Who…who are you?"

"My name is Bethany Brundridge. Are you alone?"

A moment's hesitation, then, "Ye-yes."

"Alice, can you open the door?"

"No," came a soft cry. "The door is locked."

Bethany stood for a moment, wondering how she could get Alice out of that room. Then it occurred to her that all the doors looked exactly alike. She had the heavy key to her room in her pocket. Was it possible that her key, the one in her pocket, could unlock all the other doors as well? The fortress, she reasoned, was several hundred years old. Back then, surely, there was not a different key made for every door.

She fumbled in her pocket, grabbed the key, and shoved it into the lock. Holding her breath, she turned the key.

Bethany pulled open the door and stepped into the darkened room. A young girl huddled in the middle of the floor, dressed in a monk's white robe just like the one Bethany wore. Bethany hurried toward her and sank down beside the girl she knew had to be Alice Crumley. "It is okay, Alice. Do not be afraid. As I said before, my name is Bethany Brundridge, and I have come to help you escape from these terrible people."

Alice began to cry. "Oh, miss, it's no use. They are going to kill me…an'…an'…an' now they are going to kill you too."

Bethany grabbed Alice's trembling hands. "Oh, no, they will not, Alice. I will not let them." She quickly rose to her feet and pulled Alice up with her. "But we must hurry before they find us."

Alice was now crying openly. Bethany grabbed her shoulders and shook her gently. "Listen to me, Alice. You have to be very quiet. No matter what happens, you must remain silent. Do you understand what I am saying?"

Alice, after sniffing a couple of times, nodded.

"No matter what you see or hear. If you make any sound at all, even a whimper, then they will discover us. Do you understand?"

When Alice nodded firmly, Bethany took one of her hands, turned, and started for the open door, pulling the girl behind her.

Chapter 17

Bethany was about to step down on the stair leading to the ground floor when she heard a gruff male voice. There was the sound of a scuffle, a flash of light that suddenly vanished, then the unmistakable noise of a terrible fight.

She threw up her free hand to halt her charge. "Get back, Alice," she whispered softly and pushed the young girl farther back into the room. She handed Alice their lit candle. "Here, take this and wait for me here. There is some sort of disturbance below, and I need to go see what is happening. Whatever you do, do not make a sound."

Alice grabbed at Bethany. "No! Please don't leave me," she whimpered. "I'm…I'm afraid! They're going to find me. I know it. And then they are going to kill me."

Bethany patted Alice's hand. "Oh, no, they will not. Remember what I said? I will not let them. You just need to stay back in the shadows and remain quiet. I will come back for you when I am sure there is no danger for us below." And with that, she left Alice standing there with candle in hand and visibly shaking with fear.

Without the candle to help her see, Bethany literally crept her way down each stair, clinging to the turret's wall until… A faint light reappeared in the intense darkness and she was able to see what was happening.

Two men were involved in a terrible fight. They had been blocking the light, but now she saw a torch, flickering but still lit, lying on the floor.

One of them, a huge man, wore a long white robe, like the ones she and Alice had on. The other was dressed in gentlemen's apparel and...he somehow looked familiar.

Bethany's heart nearly stopped. It was Mr. Delemere! And at the moment he was flat on his back with the big man on top of him. The robed brute held a large club in his hand and was attempting to break Mr. Delemere's hold on his wrist so he could undoubtedly bash Mr. Delemere's head in. Well, Bethany was certainly not going to let that happen. She bolted down the remaining stairs, grabbed the still-lit torch, and with all her might, she struck the robed man on the back of his head. The blow caused the torch in her hand to sputter, and for a moment Bethany thought its fire would go out. But it suddenly flared back to life just in time for her to watch the robed man slump forward to almost completely cover Phillip.

Bethany fell to her knees beside the two men. "Mr. Delemere! Whatever are you doing here? Are you all right?"

Managing to push his attacker off to one side, Phillip struggled to a sitting position. "Well, I think so, although I have a feeling I will end up with a swollen black eye. And I am almost certain I will have a matching lower lip." Gently patting the already swelling lip, he continued on. "And as for your first question, I would think the answer was obvious. I was looking for you. For some silly reason I thought it would be a good idea to save the woman I love, and plan to marry, from a terrible fate. However, it looks as though the roles have been reversed, doesn't it?"

"You know perfectly well what I mean. How—" Bethany stopped suddenly as his comment began to register. She shook a finger at him. "You, you really must stop doing that!"

Phillip managed a lopsided smile. "Doing what?"

"You just said you…"

"Yes? Go on, say it."

"You keep saying you love me. You really must stop doing that. I, I mean…how can you? You are a gentleman of quality. A member of the *ton.* You are destined to become a viscount. I am nothing but a poor vicar's daughter. I have no breeding, nor any status within polite society, and I certainly have no fortune. Why, you would be shunned within the very society you were born into, if…"

"Go on. If what?" he murmured.

"If you should marry beneath your station. Besides, you are destined to marry Elise. It is understood. Everyone says so."

Phillip rose, and helped Bethany up. But instead of releasing her, he pulled her into his arms and kissed her, completely forgetting about his bruised lip. He then whispered into her ear. "There are just two problems with all of that, Miss Brundridge. Number one, no one has asked the potential bridegroom whom he wishes to marry. And two, I am not in love with Elise, and nothing on this earth could force me to marry her. I happen to be in love with you." He released her and stepped back, becoming all business again. "Now, are you going to marry me, or not? I mean, you have to. You have seen me in nothing but my unmentionables, and I have seen you in your night rail." He chuckled softly. "And do not forget, Elise has seen both of us *dishabille* and has promised to tell the world about it. If you do not marry me, my reputation will be ruined forever. Do you want that on your conscience?"

Blushing, Bethany looked away, although she saw nothing but the image of the man she loved smiling at her.

"There is one thing I must insist upon, however."

She turned back to him. "Oh?"

"For heaven's sake, will you stop calling me 'Mr. Delemere'? My first name is Phillip, which you very well know, and I think it is high time you start using it." When her mouth curved into a soft smile, he continued on. "Yes, well, now that is settled, I recall you were about to ask me something else before I started pouring my heart out to you. What was it?"

Her smile widened. "Oh, yes. I was about to ask how you found this place, and how you knew I was here."

Phillip grinned. "Mr. Smithers. You know, Bethany, he is truly a wonder. He is a wily old fox and— But that is a long story, and we must first find the Crumley girl and get out of here before the fun begins."

Bethany looked startled, then embarrassed. "Ohhhhh! I almost forgot about Alice! I have already found her. She is upstairs, hiding. I told her to stay there until I came back for her. But what do you mean about the fun starting? What fun?"

Phillip's grin widened. "Ol' Ollie is outside, just waiting for my signal. He's got half the citizens of Newquay with him and, according to him, they are just clamoring to rescue Alice, and they intend to make short work of these heathens."

Bethany pinned him with a sly smile. "Why, Mr. De—I mean, Phillip, you are a very surprising man."

****

Many hours later, dawn was just breaking over the horizon. Phillip, back at Gull Haven, sat in one of the large wingback chairs placed in front of the salon's warm, flickering fireplace, his feet propped upon a large ottoman. A cut above one of his eyebrows had been bandaged, and just as Phillip had predicted, the area just below his injured eye was beginning to turn an ugly purple.

It had been a long and dangerous night, yet with all that had happened, Phillip was no longer tired. Regardless of his bruised lower lip, he had a contented smile on his face because he held Bethany in his arms. She was draped across his lap, her head nestled against his neck, and she was sleeping peacefully.

It seemed, now, the events that had occurred only a few hours earlier had been nothing more than a dream. After he and Bethany collected Alice, they had slipped out of the turret the same way Phillip had entered. Then, with the trio hugging the stone wall, Phillip had let out a long and powerful whistle, then waved that faithfully still burning torch, the very one Bethany had used to subdue the man trying to kill him. Exactly what happened after that was a bit of a blur.

He did recall the tall grass on the slope facing the ruins suddenly coming alive with a wave of people screaming and waving every manner of weapons, brought from their homes. Pitchforks, clubs, various forms of firearms, and more. He also recalled a couple of women suddenly appearing out of the crowd. They took hold of Alice and Bethany and quickly dragged them out and away from harm. It was a complete rout after that, and one Phillip had happily joined.

Padric and his followers did not have a chance, for they were hopelessly outnumbered and had been completely surprised, in the bargain. Only a few of the cult followers survived, and they were immediately taken into custody by Constable Barlow with the help of his assistant, Jemmy Dushay.

One last bit of information Phillip learned before starting back to Gull Haven, and perhaps the most profound: Padric Kilgallen had been killed in the mayhem. But it was not his death that made it profound. It had been the who, how, and why of his death that made it so. Charlie O'Malley had fought and stabbed Padric to death, then cut out his heart, just as Padric had done to Charlie's love, little Lucy Abney.

Phillip's thoughts scattered when Bethany stirred in his arms. She looked up at him with sleepy eyes and a secret smile on her lips. "I was dreaming about you." She sighed.

"Oh? And just what was I doing?"

"You were telling me how much you love me, and that your mother's disapproval of me is of no consequence, nor that I am only a common vicar's daughter with no money or status within society. You were telling me that you love me now, and that you always will love me. Please tell me that was not just a dream."

Phillip smiled down at her. "That was no dream, Bethany. I fell in love with you on a soft spring night, in a moonlit rose garden, and this I vow to you—I will never love another as long as I live."

It was only after Bethany had expressed the depth of her love for him, and then repeated the same vow to him, that nothing more was said for a very long time.

A word about the author…

Judith Conklin is a true Texan. She was born in Austin, Texas and grew up there. Married to a sailor, she lived a short time in California, but eventually returned to Texas.

A widow now, she lives in a small country town up in the Texas Hill Country, surrounded by ranches and handsome young cowboys who still open doors for ladies, tip their hats, and flirt outrageously with little old ladies old enough to be their grannies. Her life centers around writing, and four cats who keep her company. It is a pleasant existence, she claims, doing only what she wants, regardless of the time.

Her early years were less than pleasant, so she escaped between the pages of romance novels. The first book she ever read for pleasure was *Jane Eyre* and she was hooked. She has loved historical romances ever since, and now keeps busy writing her own.

Historical romances are not exclusive with her, however. Her first published novel was an English Gothic Romance, followed by a Western Historical Romance. *The Cornish Mystique* is her third novel. At the present time, she is finishing up a Contemporary Romantic Suspense set in Egypt during an archaeological dig, and two other English Historicals in various stages of completion.

Thank you for purchasing
this publication of The Wild Rose Press, Inc.

For questions or more information
contact us at
info@thewildrosepress.com.

The Wild Rose Press, Inc.

Milton Keynes UK
Ingram Content Group UK Ltd.
UKHW020650290424
441924UK00015B/776

9 781509 254897